THE LAST BIOGRAPHY

Robyn and Kevin Mengwasser

The reader is welcome to journal on the pages provided at the end of each chapter. The music is included to echo the story and personality of each character and can be listened to before, during, or after each chapter or the entire book.

THE LAST BIOGRAPHY
Robyn and Kevin Mengwasser
thelastbiography.com

ISBN 978-0-692-01239-0

Table of Contents

❖

The Assignment

Only one space left, one empty place on the shelf to fill. The collection had been decades in the making, and now it was almost finished. Just one more. All the planning and preparation, energy and sacrifice were culminating in perfection. There was only time and space for one more book. This would be a special book, the last biography.

A meeting was scheduled for 9:00 a.m. It was unlike any staff meeting Aaron had ever attended. He and his colleagues could sense the drama in the atmosphere with talk of a big announcement. The project was close to completion. The museum was near capacity, and soon there would be the long-awaited ceremony to dedicate a life's work and commitment. Without doubt, the owner had planned something unpredictable.

More than one generation had been guests of the Jenski Museum and had watched others as they were changed by the experience as well. They learned about the past and reflected on their own lives as they read the biographies of others. Each piece archived held special meaning for many. Hours of joy filled these halls. The museum was an extension into the community, a gift.

Its owner was highly regarded because of the contents of this acclaimed historical structure, and the famed museum was highly regarded because of its impassioned owner, Jaimin. He collected art and artifacts as well, but only those pieces which reminded him of his books, especially those where he took part

5

in the writing. Those cherished books were the focus of his attention. It consumed all his time. He started with only one, and over the years it became an incredible collection.

He wanted there to be a connection between the readers and the stories. They were to be inclusive and diverse and cover every life experience, occupation, and personality type he could conceive. There were books dedicated to the powerful and powerless. There were accounts of kings and scholars and every talent imaginable. It was important to include such variety that anyone who walked through the doors could find something that spoke to their heart. His collection was still missing something.

It was Jaimin's desire for there to be enough room for every piece of literature he could find, so he constructed a magnificent building and added to it often over the years. Resources were not an issue for him, and he spared no expense. He became so known for his unending love of books, people began helping him build his museum and add to its contents. Sometimes the additions would trickle in and sometimes they would flood.

The location of the Jenski Museum was stunning, the construction ornate, and the furnishings lavish. Because of the heirlooms it held and the vast assemblage of literature it contained, the building was as exquisite in its artistry as it was in its architecture. Having been designated and commissioned a historical landmark, upon completion and dedication its structure would no longer be altered. Having spent an immeasureable part of his life in these efforts, Jaimin knew this phase would soon be over and there would be nothing further added to the inside as well. With one more book, his purpose would be fulfilled. Jaimin had been waiting for what seemed like forever to realize the completion of his vision, and he was assured he would be present to see it all unfold.

When he first began pursuing biographies years earlier, he understood he would require help to be able to produce quality manuscripts in the quantities he desired for his collection. Numerous people assisted with the writing, and he asked an associate to secure interviews for prospective stories. This became a full-time job and, in turn, necessitated additional help. Garrick gave it everything he had. He could close this part of his career knowing he held back nothing. The plan had been in place for years, but when the timing was right, Garrick spoke to his colleagues about additional personnel. He then could be promoted to editor.

His years of experience in the field had prepared him for the intense work required, and he couldn't imagine being anywhere else. He was gifted, well known in his industry. No praise was needed but was offered readily. In time he helped fill the place with biographies. The hours spent in his office were priceless to him, and he loved every piece in the collection. It was more than a job.

Garrick also performed the role of archivist. He surveyed and processed each piece as though it was the only work of art in the museum. He had been fascinated with history and public buildings and narratives even as a youth. It was an excellent fit for the organization. The archivist in him was so concerned with the preservation of the collection, he talked to the owner about employing staff who would take great care with the truth for each piece. They would provide support and stay with the story ad infinitum. Manipulation of facts had become so prevalent, it was hard to recognize sincerity. Garrick's work could be trusted to be without embellishment. It didn't need it. It was important that he provide that reassurance through personnel.

Since Garrick was in his ultimate role and now physically located at the museum, he had the owner's blessing to send the staff to the field. Access to staff was simple because of the work already done by the editor. It was understood they were a package deal. Kecia and Aaron immediately were part of the organization. Each provided multiple skills and took on several roles and had a quality that seemed incomprehensible. Kecia had a presence about her that granted a place of solace. Aaron's gifts included thorough instruction and the ability to prompt a memory and direct it to the answer.

With more support in the field and Garrick as editor, the staff was an incredible reflection of his strength. They drew upon his character and represented him well. Garrick was delighted to be with Kecia and Aaron as they transitioned into this phase. They were with him at a critical juncture. Something that seemed impossible to everyone, they could orchestrate. All of the job requirements were met, and he had full confidence as they were sent out for interviews. This allowed him to focus where his skills were most needed.

The staff knew everything there was to know about the owner, his dreams and intentions and vision. They loved their jobs and believed so in the value of the museum, they'd do anything they were asked to assist. In all their work, the title of staff commanded the same respect as that of the owner. When they relayed information, there was no doubting its validity. Their word was solid.

Kecia and Aaron were very familiar with the collection and knew when to pursue an interview. They would speak always about the incredible artistry the editor would bring to a story. The reputation of the owner naturally flowed to the editor. It was not competitive. The owner, editor, and staff were solidly cohesive. The whole team multitasked to accomplish the goal. It was just a really great place to work. They cared for each other, and the company purpose put the challenges in perspective. The facilities were a bonus.

Staff was asked to choose candidates from their community and beyond, a story they were compelled to submit. There was urgency and yet a peace in the timing. Their jobs were not limited by rules of neutrality, and they were not prohibited from developing deep friendships. It was assumed that they would compose a list of candidates partly from individuals they already knew well. A detailed and lengthy company manual was not necessary. They were bound not by governmental laws and legal documents with signatures but by the integrity of the business and their positions within it.

No one was immune from the impact of the staff, regardless of their station in life. Kecia and Aaron knew if they became a part of these lives, they would have the same life-restoring impact they had once had with Garrick. They took their position very seriously. All of these lives had precarious directions they could take. It was understood any staff with the museum is not associated with anything that may ultimately bring harm. More than just interviewing, they were given the privilege of influencing lives.

The locations where staff would find themselves were endless, and they had amazing adventures pursuing their assignment. They were present for the highs and the lows in the process. Spontaneous long distance and difficult travel did not shake their resolve to conduct the interview and effectively support the participant. When negativity crept in, they could deal with it. They had an integral part in these lives.

Aaron's character served him well in this role. He quietly went about his work without unnecessary confrontation or a combative attitude. He ushered in a sense of hope for the future. He had spent years as a substitute teacher before taking the position with the museum. With all his gifts and characteristics, at the core Aaron was an educator. His fellow teachers would often come to him when they had questions themselves. His advice was always directed toward what is right and just. He'd find a way to help them grasp the concept at hand.

Aaron had a couple favorite subjects but was interested in most everything, so he remained a substitute rather than instructing a certain age or course of study. This allowed him also to fully utilize his ability to mentor. Students too many to count had received the benefits of his sought-after advice, even when it wasn't really what they wanted to hear. Often students would be the recipients of his poetic composition, he called it. A piece of truth would be floated by another student or family member or someone in the community, and it was pretty well known where it originated.

He was a master illustrator. If his words were too much to absorb, he knew it and even before the end of the sentence had his art pad and pencil at the ready. A simple sketch as he talked helped fill in the blanks. A student one day was greatly confused as to why a particular assignment they were to work on in class that day was relevant to not only the course but her life in general. She approached his desk with her own art pad, grabbed a pencil off the desk, and cleverly drew "Y." Well, since that really wasn't a picture, he turned the page, picked up the framed photo on the desk, and traced around it. She got it and returned his volley with a quick etching of herself in the frame, with a dreadful frown. He erased the frown, inserted a smile, and drew another empty frame.

At this point no one in the class was working. Even though they couldn't see the communication, they had never witnessed him erase and offer back the pencil. They kind of wanted to participate.

10

Aaron and his student continued their silent dialogue through several sheets of paper, both of them erasing, redrawing, not a word. It was Aaron's turn, as indicated by the pencil in his hand. He looked at the last picture, turned to the first page and scanned through the progression. He smiled and without using it, offered her the pencil. She shook her head, so he closed the book and placed the pencil back on the desk, after he replaced the spent eraser.

He motioned to her to check out the class, who still didn't know what to make of it all. She knew they deserved an explanation and proudly opened the book again and placed it into his hands. Aaron went to the board and retraced the entire incident. Somehow she had gotten from "Y" to a picture representing "This is what I believe I am to do with my life." She wasn't the crying type or she would have reached for the tissue. She did look visibly relieved, not because she was amazed he didn't simply send her to the office. It wouldn't have been her first journey down that hall. She was just overwhelmed this had turned into something so useful. She was even more excited when she saw Aaron place his own art pad on an old music stand nearby and extend the pencil to the class.

One by one, each of them took their turn. This went on for a week. It wasn't required for points in class participation or scored as a percentage of their comprehensive grade. They wanted in on this. Of course, the one student who knew since toddlerhood what he was destined to become went first. Good thing, because a major portion of the class needed until at least day two to come up with something, anything.

The eraser and responsive drawing was offered not just to the teacher but all members of the class. Young men and women symbolically talked more that week than they had in months. Cliques dissolved. Those who had a sense of their future got honest feedback, helpful criticism, and encouragement. Those with no idea discovered abilities they themselves hoped they had and everyone else knew they had. Even the decided student who went first added to his plans.

Day three brought a twist when a student lacking confidence in his artistry closed the art pad and set his piggy bank on the desk, indicating his desire to be a banker. In response, stuff flew out of backpacks and off shelves to the point where the desk looked like lost and found accumulated since birth.

The last student of the week went to the front of the class with his coat, hat, and gloves. He put them on and went out the door. The class had gotten so good at this, it didn't make sense to them not to retrieve theirs from their lockers and return to the hall. He led them all outside to two trees. He had gotten permission to run an extension cord to the evergreen, which he had decorated with lights, and he had a blanket wrapped around the deciduous. It was clear he firmly believed he was to care for a tree nursery, so in affirmation, a student returned a fallen pinecone to its proper ornamental place, and another had one of those flower pens that she disassembled and gave to the bare tree as an early bloom.

The whole week had been responsive, and they wished they could respond to one field trip with another, but they did get in a quick snowball fight before returning to the rest of their classes. It was nothing new. It was classic show and tell, object lesson, and field trip stuff. The methods were ancient. But, to this class it was special and something that they would reflect on individually during critical times in their life. They could also scale it down to get through a crucial moment.

This was supposed to be speech class, and hardly a word was uttered all week. Aaron updated the teacher upon her return the following week. She laughed uncontrollably and explained what a difficult time she had had getting this bunch to relax. The exercise was very relevant to an upcoming assignment, and she was sure it was good preparation for them. She assumed they might need an "only words" day in her mission to help them be comfortable with public speaking and with all forms of communication. She would incorporate this success into her teaching, especially with this class, but may request the same time off next year and ask for the same substitute.

His pupils loved their ability to communicate with Aaron using anything, anytime, anyplace, for no reason at all. More than one parent upon hearing of his methods went immediately to the art store for an art pad and big eraser. The mayor got wind of it and wanted to send the template to the council, press, and maybe the U.N. while he was at it. At the end of the year, the class put together a book for Aaron titled "No Words." Everyone contributed a page.

When Aaron took the position at the museum, he knew he wasn't leaving teaching. He had been and would be a teacher. That talent would be exploited in this new assignment, as well as many other talents he possessed. He was prepared to use them all to help in the collection of biographies that would mean so much to the team, the museum, and all who entered. He believed it was what he was to do with his life.

Kecia held several positions over the years, mostly in personnel. She didn't know how to wake up on the wrong side of the bed. Every place she touched became permeated with joy. If you could somehow test it on a happiness meter, the cheerfulness left in her wake was off the chart. She was straightforward, uncomplicated, and handled arduous tasks with ease. Kecia was all about the stuff that lasts. She had a way with life and rubbed off on everyone around her, with this uncanny ability to flit in and out of lives at the right time. She was simply a delight to have on the team. Any organization would be lucky to have dozens just like her.

One of her favorite activities in her spare time was to reconnect with the individuals she had personally worked with whose biographies were already included in the archives. She fondly remembered her very first interview, and when still possible, she would contact her previous aspirants and talk about their current circumstances. Kecia loved seeing and hearing them talk so positively about something she felt privileged to support.

She recalled watching many of them vacillate between euphoria and fear, elation at just the thought of the invitation to be a part of this place that received such high praise, and fear of not being book-worthy. There were never regrets in choosing to participate, even in such a public endeavor. Their conversations usually resulted in laughter rather than worry over admittedly conspicuous flaws. They valued the opportunity as a gift.

Kecia adored a grand party and purposed to go completely out of her way to ensure that all of the people she had come into contact with through her years in this position were invited to celebrate the owner's accomplished collection. That the dedication was imminent was exhilarating to the entire team. She supposed if you listened intently, you could probably hear the excitement within the stately walls of their beloved Jenski.

The owner had asked his editor to complete just one more biography. Garrick's heart pounded as he walked by the place where the last book was to go. He experienced this every time he began a new project, but this was different. The dream of his finished work would propel him through the process.

Jaimin opened the doors to the conference room with great resolution. His team was present, and as anticipated, he announced, "This is it! This will be the last biography. After all of these years working together, we're so close to accomplishing this dream. We'll interview for and edit and place on the shelf just one more biography before the dedication we've been longing to experience together."

Each member of the team looked forward to their new roles they would fulfill during and after the dedication. With all of the excitement, they couldn't possibly sit and dialogue and discuss details in the conference room without feeling compelled to tour the museum and reflect on its contents. They reviewed and reminisced, greeted and spoke with guests, and talked of possibilities. Jaimin especially adored the unexpected.

Aaron and Kecia were each given a journal and invited to use it if prompted. They could record their responses or thoughts during this process or use it to remember attributes and characteristics, circumstances, struggles, and experiences important in relaying why the story deserved to be selected. It could help them stay focused by releasing to paper what was consuming their hearts amidst the anticipation.

They would be asked for their recommendation and their choice. They were to forward information regarding each applicant and continue interviewing until the owner had received seven applications from which to choose whose story would be their last biography. Kecia and Aaron would find a balance between thoroughness and urgency.

The reader of this book is welcome to journal as well on the pages provided at the end of each chapter. The music is included to reflect the story and personality of each character and can be listened to before, during, or after each chapter or the entire book.

Journal

❖

Peter

It had been years since his company dissolved, and Peter had moved away physically and emotionally to hinder any potential reminder of the effect it had had on his employees. His business went under when a company he had partnered with through several business cycles solicited a competitor and contracted with Peter's largest client. He later learned that there had been illegal payoffs involved but couldn't prove it in time to save his business. The client ultimately realized what had taken place, filed a complaint, and took its business elsewhere.

Of course he had different plans for his own future that did not develop, but what concerned him most was the abrupt way he had to release his help. A number of the 12 individuals had worked for him the entire 20 years his business existed. He sold his company assets and distributed them as fairly as he could but still felt horrible that he had not tightened up his contracts and business relationships so as not to alter so many lives. He was generally a cautious and careful person. His trusting nature unfortunately in this situation trumped those qualities.

Peter had always taken the peaceful road. It never entered his mind to confront. There were times in his life when it would have been better had he dealt with some issues in relationships or work performance, but it was not in his nature. There were also times when he was grateful that he did not wrestle with needing to make things right. How could he? He wondered how he had been able to lead in his business without possessing the ability to directly address pressing concerns, but he must have attracted a certain personality who is drawn to the gift of letting each individual self-examine. His presence and example was often all it took, and he delighted in the outcome when he saw someone take responsibility, learn and grow, without him saying a word.

In the loss of his own business, however, his inability to confront did not serve him well. For years he wished he had exercised some form of righteous indignation even though he knew it would not have changed the immediate outcome. Addressing the wrongdoing for what it was would have made his employees feel more supported and could have possibly averted further wrongdoing by the same entity. It would have prevented this from infecting his soul for all these years.

Peter had investigated and researched and pursued every avenue he could think of to undo the damage. His client had taken advantage of his integrity and manipulated the circumstances. Loyalty perhaps was a lost quality. In the end what benefited a few but devastated many somehow justified the disrespect to colleagues and friends. They call it business.

Was it pride that kept him from facing this? He was relieved he was in a different city than the client and understood how the circumstances affected his decision to even move from his own city. He never really wanted to attend another professional convention even though he had made many good friends and was now in a position to be a mentor. He used to love having people around all the time, so the transition was difficult. He questioned his own take on the whole situation. Maybe it wasn't as unscrupulous as he felt it was and he was too emotionally tied to be neutral.

Peter knew the loss of his company had affected Kecia deeply. She worked there only a few months in administration before the closure but was dedicated and a bright spot in everyone's day. He was concerned for her, but she seemed to understand the big picture and how it affected everyone. There were people whose lives were altered greatly by the selfishness of a few. It was devastating to a lot of people she cared about, and it was completely unnecessary. The market at the time was good.

She could see the potential long-term damage and knew ultimately it would catch up to the company who seemingly was profiting at the time. Caring for the industry as a whole and the people she grew to know who would be impacted, she approached and confronted the owner of that company. It wasn't at all brave; it was just the right thing to do. In a sense, she was warning them of the eventual harm they would cause to themselves. No entity rolls over another without inevitable repercussions. Peter did not know that Kecia had gone to this effort to try to help him save his business.

Throughout his life he learned to put all his efforts toward business and leave other things alone. That was a wise course for him. Had he not learned that skill, he would have filled his head with the rights and wrongs of not only his relationships but all of humanity. The fairness factor would have consumed him. Peter was able to tuck all that away and reserve his need for a state of equilibrium to things he could control. It became a talent. The books balanced, and he was able to play the roles required of him in all the other areas of his life.

He took care of pending business details daily. It was a skill he learned early in life, and he had practiced this at his company long enough to make it a habit, so it seeped into the way he lived. This trait he possessed worked well as he exited and entered different phases. It also caused substantial discontent over this whole episode that he couldn't put to rest.

He had not been interested in exploring the long-term effects of any of his actions. He knew there was plenty of noble contribution, but he was also intimidated by the losses he may have caused. He had put his lost business on the shelf for years and never really healed but was now at a place in his life where he felt the need to wrap up unfinished business.

Peter didn't know how to accomplish this or how to even begin but knew the timing was right when he received a phone call from his beloved former employee. "Peter, it's Kecia! I think of you often. Are you and Amy enjoying your retirement?"

He was so surprised and excited to hear from her that he hollered across the room, "Amy, it's Kecia!"

"When can you visit us?"

"I'd love to see you! I'm also working on an incredible project and would like to talk to you about it. What does your calendar look like?"

"Are you kidding? We're retired. When can you make it?"

"Next week?"

"Honey, Kecia is visiting next week!"

"Let us know as soon as you have details, and we'll pick you up at the airport. Stay as long as you can."

The exchange was so quick, Peter didn't have a chance to catch his breath or collect his thoughts, until the phone hit the receiver. All the memories replayed again. There were lots of good ones, but the ending always tainted them. More than a tinge of fear developed as he thought about the prospect of reminiscing during this visit. There was also anger, not just that this had happened but that it continued to dominate what otherwise was a successful career. There was just a week to put his thoughts in order, as much as he could do so on his own. Kecia could help with the rest.

The reunion was everything hoped for and more than anticipated. They all stayed up late into the night reconnecting. The conversation was light, what the kids and grandkids were doing, how they each filled their days.

Kecia talked briefly about her work with the Jenski Museum but wanted to wait until everyone was rested before pursuing it further. She was anxious to present this incredible opportunity to him but also understood he was as much in a different place emotionally as he was now physically since he had not returned for even a brief visit after moving away. No plans were made for the next day, so a leisurely afternoon would be perfect timing to discuss her assignment.

Amy busied herself in the kitchen to give Kecia and Peter a chance to talk. Kecia began telling him about some of his previous employees and how they had gained valuable experience at his company that they were now utilizing in their current work. This was completely unexpected for Peter. All this time he was just sure there was more damage than good and more negative than positive impact.

Kecia was pretty well-connected in the community and knew the direction that everyone took after the company dissolved. She spoke only of a few of her colleagues because she wanted Peter to see directly the growth these lives experienced because of their work with him. She could talk about it endlessly, but to show him would speak volumes. She so hoped he and Amy would agree to accompany her back home.

Peter opened up, "I've really had a hard time letting this go. Seeing you, I can't help but think of all the wonderful and productive years with my company I had wished for you and for all the others. This highlights the feelings I have tried unsuccessfully to diminish for so long now. It was the one thing I felt I did really well. I love my family intensely, and I've had a great life, but this was my project. For years it was my identity, and it failed; I failed. Us old guys have too much time to spend reflecting and wondering what if and asking what about."

Her reply was insightful. "I know this about you. That's part of the reason for the visit, and I believe part of the reason why I was given a position working for you years before this visit. Even if you were not an old guy, you never could leave the office with anything in your 'in' basket. It's okay that things have to be just so for you. All these years of carrying this, I'm sure it has been awful."

"Kecia, it's also the resentment I feel towards the parties involved, business in general, and sometimes everyone and everything around me."

"Well, look at the world today. How much of the turmoil is a result of greed? An industry gets caught up in gouging, and ultimately the tables turn."

Peter responded in agreement, "I can't help but think if everyone took a small part of the responsibility, this whole mess would be over by now. I wouldn't want to be the one to decide who gets let go so that everyone else can stay at their current level. It reminds me of birds following a fishing boat. They're all so noisy and rude. There are enough resources. This country produces twice the food it needs. There is enough medicine, there is enough transportation, there's enough clothing and shelter. If our country can do it, others can as well. There would be enough if greed did not exist."

She knew it wouldn't be sufficient to only tell him of some of the awesome things that had happened to those he felt were profoundly affected. A few of their friends of many years had made the trip to see the couple, but Amy and Peter had never been back home. They left an incredible amount of history and memories. Their children were now located in different parts of the country, but the years of raising them left reminders in every nook and cranny of the community. Amy especially missed reliving those memories. She had longed to go back frequently but waited patiently, hoping there would be time for him to heal.

Kecia believed their visit would be more than welcomed and had sought the appropriate timing to get in touch. She knew this invitation in person would be more compelling. "I think it might help you process this if you and Amy come back with me to see the amazing legacy you have established. You're letting one event define your existence, and the truth doesn't even remotely match your fears." There was doubt on his face but also determination, and he agreed to talk with his wife. Clearly he already knew her answer.

"Oh, Kecia, I've been so self-centered, talking about all of these things that focus on my life. You said on the phone you were involved with something extraordinary. I had heard you were working with the Jenski, and I'm elated you found something so fulfilling. Tell me about your project."

"You know I love listening to your heart, and I'll have an even greater opportunity to do so if you allow me to include you in my work. I haven't talked a lot about it yet because I didn't want to overwhelm you with my assignment."

Peter didn't know her job responsibilities at the museum but had been there before, and he saw the look on her face. He was sure the doubt on his face grew, but he felt safe around Kecia and trusted her judgment. "So which do I want to know first, what you're up to or what you are asking of me?"

"Well, either way. Just don't come to a conclusion out loud or in your head right away, or until you've heard more, and probably not until after you've had a chance to go back home.

I've been interviewing for potential stories. I love this part of my work. The biography section is almost complete. We've added shelves wherever possible, but it's stuffed. There's one space left, and the owner announced there's really only time for one more. I'd like to submit you as a candidate. We'll be interviewing several.

"I know, I know. Take a breath. Take your time. Ask for Amy's input. Leave the door open."

He wasn't sure if this whole biography thing was something he even wanted to undertake. There was only one spot and several interviews, and it would be displayed in a public and prominent place. He wasn't really into reality TV. He found it to be self-absorbed and the furthest thing from realistic. But he also found himself watching, frequently. What was the draw? He didn't care for when the participants were critical of each other. Sometimes the hype was beyond overdramatic and the scripted long pauses completely transparent. The whole process seemed a little silly.

However, he did understand something meaning a great deal to someone even if the rest of the world couldn't comprehend it. For him the intrigue was just finding out what happened to everyone involved. It reminded him of how he felt when he sat down to watch a sporting or news event. The fact that it was unpredictable kept his attention. It wasn't just simply who won but all the circumstances that led up to the victory. He felt it enriched his life to watch others live out theirs.

Peter was intrigued. He also wondered if he had anything to offer. The museum was held in very high regard, and he only wanted to participate if he could add something significant or something that may help others if they read the finished piece. He wanted to learn something himself through his involvement.

It was too hard to see himself on the shelf, yet what an honor! Maybe it would give purpose to his pain and loss. Isn't that what people sometimes naturally do after experiencing tragedy? If they can share the mistake or trial and somehow prevent another such event, or counsel and grieve with individuals who have befallen the same tragedy, it often provides purpose and healing for all involved.

He didn't design or construct or model or cook, sing or dance. He did not want a new job, and he certainly didn't want a new mate. He wasn't a wilderness adventurer, and his life was not interesting or unique enough to capture it all on camera. He wasn't the smartest, funniest, wealthiest, most handsome, most athletic, most anything. This seemed different than all of that. Whether there was a grand prize or consolation package, he connected with the thought of a legacy. He could have his life edited and archived with this respected collection, and someone might be able to learn from his struggles.

He was not fully committed, but he was fascinated. Amy's opinion was important to him. She was not pushy, controlling, or a nag. She stood by him in the most difficult parts of his life, and she saw the value that this would bring. He wanted to do something significant and meaningful with his whole life but especially with these years. He consented to return home and leave this door open.

They all three made the trip back home together. Kecia asked them to contact her in a couple days after they were settled. Amy had made arrangements for them to stay with friends. The emotions were indescribable as their friends drove them around town, stopping at every location that held special meaning. Everything had changed and nothing had changed. It looked much different, but it all felt the same.

Peter was ready. Amy had frequently helped out in the office and also planned any social events, so she knew his employees and their families well. She too was interested in the direction their lives had taken, and her support was both invited and welcomed. Kecia first drove them to a large medical supply business. She introduced herself at the front desk and explained they were there for their appointment with Brad.

Brad was Peter's first employee and the person he would put in charge when he had to be out of the office. He was competent and loyal and great with people. He greeted Peter and Amy with a hug.

Peter was grateful to see him looking so well. "I have missed you! Tell me about your life and your work."

"The kids are in college now. Can you imagine? My wife works here as well." He winked as he finished his thought, "She doesn't work in my department, though. We all still golf together whenever we can."

Peter noticed Brad's nameplate outside his office door and glanced that direction. "Brad, I'm sorry."

Brad interrupted, "Before you continue, I remember how many times you said those words years ago. You did everything you could. It only took a short time to find work, and the time I was off was when our oldest was ill, so I was fortunate to be there to care for him. I received important experience with your company, worked here in several departments, and took extra training. We have three buildings here, research and development, manufacturing and testing, marketing and administrative. Let me show you this manufacturing and testing building that I manage."

They all got the grand tour. Peter could sense the great level of respect Brad commanded with his personnel. Before leaving, Peter decided to finish his thought from their earlier conversation. "I'm changing my two words that I spoke to you from 'I'm sorry' to 'I'm proud,' Brad." They exchanged contact information, instructions to get in touch when time permitted, and another round of hugs.

Peter got the impression that Kecia could probably repeat this scenario all day, and he was now more than ready. The next visit was to Marcus, who was gifted in sales. He now ran the local food bank. "Hey, I heard you guys were back in town. It's so great to see you."

"What is my sales expert doing giving things away all day?"

"Well, ironically, every time the shelves are empty, I'm in sales. Every time I dream up a fundraiser or contest or something-a-thon, I'm in sales. Every time I ask for a donation, I'm in sales. I get to ask for it, and I get to give it away. How colossal is that? It's amazing I haven't asked you yet! Come take a look at our photo book of some of the events we've held and the people we've been able to help."

Peter recognized his gift on every page. They not only fed people locally but organized contributions for disasters across the country and to the other side of the world. It never occurred to him until now that it would have been selfish to shelter these talented individuals under his care through all these years.

After lunch the final visit of the day was to the police station. Peter was trying to guess which of his previous employees would be at this location, and what the possible connection could be to his former business. Law enforcement was not at all related. When he saw John, it still didn't make sense. John had been Peter's accountant. Maybe he worked with the budget or was somehow involved with the union. No, that's a uniform and badge, and that's definitely a gun and handcuffs, the entire package.

The conversation was brief yet reflective. John had just a short time before a department meeting. It was cordial and positive but not informative like the last two stops had been, and Peter couldn't see anything at all that he may have done to advance John's career. He was doing well and serving his community, but he wasn't using any skills acquired with Peter's help. What was the connection?

Kecia led Peter and Amy down a hallway lined with framed documents, pictures, and awards. She stopped at John's. "If I had asked him, he would have been too humble to talk about it." Peter got it. There was a picture of an entire family John and his partner were responsible for saving, which wouldn't have happened had he still been employed with Peter. To see a huge amount of good with lasting value from something he felt so awful about, his heart was lifted.

"I spoke to you about four of your employees when I visited your home, and we just looked in on three others. You thought it was devastating, and it was for a while, but both the experience gained under your leadership and the actual closing of the company opened doors for every last one of them. Would you like to see or hear about the remaining five?"

He laughed and responded, "You know, Amy has no fewer than half a dozen friends who have granted us an open invitation to stay as long as we would like, and we've had such a great time being here, we'd like to stay and spend as much time as we can renewing temporarily lost but not forgotten relationships. I appreciate all your efforts to help in this process, but if you've got a list -- and I'm sure you do -- with phone numbers and addresses, we are eager to reconnect on our own with all of them."

His demeanor changed as he continued, "I do believe there's something else I need to do."

Kecia understood. Peter knew he needed to address the owner of the company he had partnered with that was responsible for the business closing, who was no longer in business himself due to his professional reputation. Kecia felt it was the right time to tell him how she had tried to reason with his former partner before this was final. She had a grasp on the situation but received so much defiance and friction, there was no opportunity to talk about all of the people he was negatively affecting with his take-over. It was clear he had made his decision, and no level-headed insight would help.

Peter told Kecia, "I missed the opportunity to make sure this damage never happens to anyone else. I know it wouldn't have changed his mind, but my help sure would have appreciated it had I confronted him. I should have told my story, and the point now is not to remake the past but to be able to move forward."

Peter was replete with the ideology he and Kecia had discussed as he confronted the owner of the company that solicited his competitor. He approached him on his own and simply stated, "It was wrong, and you're forgiven." What more needed to be said? It didn't matter whether he conceded his wrongdoing. This could finally be put to rest.

This process of studying deeply the reality of the past, with the guidance of Kecia, brought Peter an overwhelming sense of clarity and ability to address his industry in particular and business as a whole. He wrote anonymously to a business magazine detailing his story, hoping still to prevent damage by anyone else in the future. He thought to submit it to his professional journal but knew it would be perceived as directed only to the company who had personally done him harm.

Submitting it anonymously to a general business magazine was appropriate and useful.

Kecia met again with Peter and Amy after they had a chance to dialogue, sort through their thoughts, and make some decisions. Peter began, "Thank you. These last few days have brought much-needed closure."

"There is just one more element to this," Kecia responded.

"The universe rolls along and I can't fix it?"

"Pretty much. You didn't intend for this to happen, and even if you did, even if it was malicious and nothing good resulted and every last person attached to the episode suffered from it, one dark event does not define you. This all stems from the fact that you care so much, which in the right venue is a coveted quality, but it can also prey upon you. Your employees are fine, you dealt with the offense, but you haven't forgiven yourself yet. This opened a door for you as well. You weathered the storm. It was tough for a while, but everyone involved learned of new opportunities because of your building blocks. Some took a week, others longer, and now it is your turn. Because of your time invested and the depth to which you have given of yourself, your opportunity is great."

Kecia took the time to help Peter see how something that he hoped was just okay had become something good and would continue to grow. He had seen this in his life before and with so many others, but with this situation, resolution had evaded him. Peter thought he was not unlike most of humanity with a few things gnawing at their own novel. Maybe there was a failed relationship that they had hoped at the end of their life would be intact. Perhaps a bad decision was made in their work or in their finances, or a blunder on some athletic field or court or rink. The losses are huge for someone known for one thing. How can there be a failure in image?

Who really can compensate for losses in this life? The feeble attempts at lawsuits and a chance to speak of an injustice, even when the truth wins, does not reverse the tide. People determine to live long enough to make it to court, and countless victims have stayed up all hours of the night writing the speeches they will give. Families wait together at executions, hoping somehow a last-minute acknowledgment might diminish the pain of the loss.

Peter was prepared to give Kecia his answer concerning her request to submit his story for the museum. He knew his circumstances were relevant. How many businesses and industries take a hit because of the greed of a few? It snowballs in this global economy. He experienced the gift of being at zero before the end of his life and having everything that seemed to matter become null. Words that he thought were lost flowed from his voice. He really believed this.

He appreciated the art of listening in his relationships. There was no opinionated conversation or lectures from Kecia, though she had wisdom and was in a position to offer it. Just her presence brought out Peter's ability to see the truth, and accept the need to speak it. He could do so without prompting, so it became his truth. To him it was the only time it counted, when he owned it. He wanted that to stick around and be a part of who he was forever.

As he had thought about all the years he had spent cowering, he became angry. How many people in their lives had faced this? He'd watched countless people do so many good things, make a mistake, and then be known the rest of their lives for the mistake. Nobody has the market on a difficult life. Whether intentional or not, reckless or not, blatantly wrong or not, it was upsetting to see the weight he and the rest of the world placed on an error, allowing it to ruin all the good. He refused to believe this lie for himself and through his biography might help others avoid years of endless pain.

He clutched Amy's hand as he happily declared, "My story does have meaning and purpose, and I can't imagine not sharing it with you and hopefully many others."

At even the slightest glance, the contentment that had been missing so long in his life was clearly evident on Peter's face. Too much of his life had been spent toiling when goodness and rest and great happiness is so readily available. Who wouldn't want this freedom?

It thrilled Kecia to send an e-mail and update her editor with some of the details of Peter's story. Garrick was ecstatic that the applications were starting to arrive. He especially appreciated receiving this one so he could begin his processing.

Kecia believed she could comprehend how Jaimin would respond to this candidate. She was hugely perceptive even with Jaimin's ability to come up with something inconceivable. Peter had spent a considerable amount of time devoted to his vocation as well, and she knew Jaimin would understand.

After returning home, Peter experienced something he had not in years. Whether awake or resting, a new dream was taking place in his soul. He thought he was too old to dream, for he was retired and content, mostly.

Journal

Adlai

With one candidate enrolled, Kecia possessed a high level of enthusiasm to submit as many entrants as possible before one was chosen. This individual would be very different from her previous undertaking. Adlai was only seven years old, and she lived right across the street. Adlai hoped she would never move away. She loved herself from A to Z when she was with Kecia, who gladly supported her adventures.

She adored gardening with her father and playing dress-up with her mother. They encouraged her creativity and development by telling her to share her ideas and then run with them. Frequently her brother solicited her help with his science projects. She was his faithful assistant. No question seemed ridiculous to her even if the reaction was otherwise, and very few opportunities were missed to tell others of her love for life. When she had an idea, even though it was thought of as silly by a well-meaning adult, she knew it was a good idea. Everything was pure and honest and void of heavy societal pressures.

Many evenings she would arrive at Kecia's home to play their favorite game of "Well, why not?" It didn't matter whose idea it was. Both without hesitation were ready to participate. Sometimes these outings were used as a tool to pour valuable life lessons into Adlai's sweet, receptive heart. Sometimes it was discovered those values were already there.

Their first encounter occurred just a few months previous to Kecia's recent assignment, shortly after Adlai's family moved into their new home across the street. It took Adlai all of a week to scope out the entire block for any potential new friends and to determine their routine schedules. She was glad when Kecia arrived at their house one evening with the traditional plate of welcoming cookies because she included Kecia at the top of her list of friends she would like to make.

"Mom, can I take her to see the sky?"

It was the time of the evening that everyone enjoys, the sunset, but Adlai's focus was different from the rest of the world's. She appreciated the sun low in the sky and the colors of any clouds reflecting off of it, but her favorite part was the horizon after the rest of the spectacle had already elapsed. Her mother was trying to read Kecia's expression to see whether she needed to gently intervene and suggest perhaps another time. Kecia without reservation exclaimed, "Well, why not?"

And so it began. Off the two went with some of the cookies and a new friendship. Even though she was the new kid on the block, she already knew the best hillside to view creation's show. They watched the setting and reflecting, and then when everyone else would have gone home, Adlai insisted they linger.

"Do you see it? Look just above the trees. It's red. Then it lightens and turns kind of orange, then yellow. Next is green, blue, and purple. The whole sky is a rainbow!"

"Oh, I do see it! Amazing! I love a good rainbow."

Kecia thought she could share some boring scientific explanation or perhaps her own personal interpretation of what they were witnessing, but the moment was too perfect as it was. As they returned home, she asked Adlai if she would like to come to her home some evening and bake cookies together. Not surprisingly, Adlai asked, "Can we make some for the whole block?" They looked at each other and giggled and spoke in unison, "Well, why not?"

Their marathon baking session, cookie delivery, and meet and greet required a Saturday to complete. It was a terrific way for Adlai to introduce herself to everyone on her list of friends. There was one home where she had not been able to determine who lived there and what their daily activities were. As lively as Adlai was, she could also be very gentle. Kecia was eager to see her response to Mrs. Benson, a woman in her later years without family nearby. She herself had looked in on her occasionally and helped her with tasks she was unable to complete alone.

It wasn't too long after they were invited in when Adlai began working on things she noticed needed done, and then before they left, her giving young spirit couldn't help but arrange to visit every Thursday evening and assist with any projects she could. After only two weeks she organized a work evening with all her new friends on the block. Arriving with many plates of cookies, they cleaned and cooked, took care of the dishes and laundry, and worked on the yard. And why not?

Kecia noticed it was the time of year when frequently a flock of birds could be seen leaving together to prepare for the next season. She thought it was a great occasion for one of their life lessons and anticipated Adlai would arrive at her home within a few days for their next adventure. When she heard the familiar knock on the door, she was tickled pink because she already had the evening planned.

They went to their favorite hillside and just sat. It wasn't close to sunset, so Adlai's level of curiosity was overwhelming. Patience was not her most abundant characteristic, and, well, she was only seven, so every time she saw something new or even thought she saw something new, every time the wind blew a blade of grass one direction or the other, she exclaimed, "That's it!"

Kecia grinned and quietly stated, "Wait, wait and nothing else."

It seemed like hours of waiting and nothing else, but it couldn't have been, for there was still no sunset. Adlai began to wonder if the setting sun was what she was eventually supposed to see and the reason Kecia started looking so early was to have an opportunity to show the fun of patience. It's not a tactic her parents had ever tried before, but they had certainly talked about her not being very patient.

As Kecia had hoped, a flock of birds finally entered the picture. They dipped several feet simultaneously to avoid power lines and then just as effortlessly elevated to their previous level of flight. Kecia repeated the question Adlai first asked of her at their inaugural friendship event. "Do you see it?"

"Well, yeah. That's the most action we've seen for hours!"

Since it took Kecia a while to stop laughing enough to be able to respond, by the time she asked the question again, the birds could no longer be seen. Adlai wanted to hit rewind and replay. She expected at the least another flock to arrive so she could be sure she saw everything and would know how to answer appropriately.

"I saw a bunch of birds fly that direction and almost run into a bunch of wires."

"The way they flew together, that's how everything is supposed to look when people work together, when everybody is on the same page."

"Oh, you mean what do I really see, like the rainbow!"

"Absolutely!"

The field trip had been a success. Kecia trusted that this would be a powerful visual reminder for many of Adlai's opportunities to learn. She could picture her thinking about this evening when faced with leadership issues, confrontation and reconciliation, the importance and beauty of relationship and family, respect for unity. The notion that all of these things could be seen only after a period of waiting was just a delightful plus in how their excursion unfolded. It would be easy for Adlai to believe in the incredible universe, especially after taking in everything Kecia had to show her.

Often when Adlai couldn't find words to say how she was feeling, she repeated some of the things Kecia had told her. They had talked so much, and Kecia's expressions and concepts couldn't help but flow. She no doubt was too young to understand copyright or plagiarism or giving appropriate credit. She just knew how right the words were. She would understand later in life how many precarious positions were avoided because of her words and also why sometimes it actually created a ruckus.

Adlai was busy many evenings with her friends, but whenever time permitted, she spent time with Kecia. Adlai's mother contacted Kecia one evening and invited her over while the children were spending time at their friends' homes. She and her husband wanted to make sure that their daughter was not requiring too much of Kecia's time. She assured them that she had all kinds of time to spend with such an inspirational soul, and they often completed tasks together that she otherwise would not have accomplished on her own.

Kecia also took this opportunity to tell Adlai's parents about the work at the museum and the excitement surrounding their latest assignment. She explained how honored she would be to enter Adlai as a possible choice for the last biography, and she assured them that because of Adlai's age, the museum would protect her identity.

Adlai's parents both had spent many memorable days at the Jenski Museum and were in awe at the request presented to them. It was all her father could do to keep his emotions in check as he answered.

"We've been so grateful for your involvement in our daughter's life. Parents could expend every last ounce of energy they have being the best role models they can envision, and the children would still need to see it from someone else. I've even been able to learn from Adlai.

"We can love them, but they believe we don't have a choice. She feels your choice to love her. You have done so much good together, and she comes home with these fabulous tales. The only difficulty is getting her to go to bed after the exhilarating telling and reliving of all your shared activities.

"Even though the two of you are spending time together, we grow fonder of you by watching her. I hear these values from her, and I can just imagine you found some subtle way to allow her to pick them up and claim them as her own. Listening to you, I hear her, and listening to her, I hear you."

Kecia was beyond her usual joyous self. "I also hear the two of you in her. She has some of your finest traits, and she has learned more from you than you can comprehend. I believe there is a little bit of everyone in a little bit of everyone. I'm certain you were given the gift of a loving mentor as well.

"A child needs more attention than you can give. A parent needs more perfection than they can offer. A professor needs more wisdom, a doctor needs more answers, a philanthropist needs more resources. I believe it's by design that we all need something more than what is directly in front of us. It keeps us pursuing and searching and dreaming."

The whole concept was still completely overwhelming for her parents. "We're so proud of her. We'd like to tell the entire planet about her, but she hasn't climbed to the highest mountaintop or flown solo around the world. It's such a special place, and it's the last book."

With full confidence, Kecia laid aside their inhibitions. "She's an extraordinary child, a remarkable little girl. Every child deserves to be represented, and she would handle that well. A faulty old myth asserted that children were to be seen and not heard, but they are to be heard. They have a voice and unencumbered opinions, and their minds are developing. They are finding a place where they belong. They are to be celebrated and remembered and applauded."

Adlai's father proudly responded, "We'd be honored to have you include her as a candidate. I think we all know what her answer will be, but you have our blessing to ask."

Kecia had taken Adlai to the museum on one of their first outings. Oh, she could have stayed forever. She had just as many questions as replies. It was too hard not to interrupt with all the excitement going through her head. The day ended far too soon, but their friendship became timeless.

Kecia had pursued every morsel of information to the finest detail that the owner had in place. She did so in order to impart this to everyone. Of course this would be given to all of the candidates, but to Adlai it felt like a big sister sharing all of her deepest secrets. The evening after receiving her parents' blessing, Kecia didn't wait for Adlai to show up for their field trip. This day she was found knocking on Adlai's door with a question to ask. She was too excited to wait to share details of the incredible day they would travel to the Jenski Museum with the rest of the group to experience history in the making.

"Do you remember when I took you to the Jenski Museum and we went to the room with all the books about different people?" Adlai nodded in agreement. "You had such a hard time figuring out which one you wanted to read."

"There were too many to decide."

"What if I told you there's only room for one more book?"

"Oh, I'd believe that. There were way too many to decide."

Kecia felt certain it would not be difficult at all for Adlai to know that it would be great fun to take part in this activity, but she still found her answer to the next question completely amusing.

"Well, what if I told you that could be your book?"

"Oh, I've already written a book, and I have a book club. Would you like to be a member?"

This approach to life was refreshing. "I'd love to be a member! Wow, if you've already written a book and have your very own book club, wouldn't it be great to have a book all about you next to all those other books we saw at the museum?"

"Well, why not? Who wouldn't want to be in the Jenski Museum?"

That was the answer they all expected. She was too young to have done anything so significant as to be a life lesson for all those to follow, but she was fascinating and delightful, and her gift would be some light reading in a collection sometimes full of complication. She would be an awesome contender! Kecia telephoned Garrick to tell him about Adlai. He was pleased to hear from her so soon after receiving her last application.

Their next outing Kecia told her all about entering her story with the museum. "Adlai, you remind people to return to the days when all things are possible. Everything can be undone and redone. You encourage them to look at things with the freshness of youth and the wisdom of experience, to retrain thoughts and habits against the misperceptions picked up along the way."

Adlai glowed when Kecia told her that these words came directly from the owner of the museum.

Journal

Matthew

"Hello."

"May I speak with JoAnne or Rick, please?"

"This is JoAnne."

"Good morning. My name is Aaron. I was one of Matthew's teachers in high school."

"Oh, I remember him speaking of you. He adored being in your class."

"We all knew he would do something incredible with his life."

"Thank you."

"I'm with the Jenski Museum now, and I'd like to talk to you and your husband about Matthew's story. I also have something that I think you may appreciate."

"We'd be thrilled to talk with you."

"May I visit you some evening this week?"

JoAnne paused to glance at their calendar. They were available this evening and the next, but she wanted to give Rick time to prepare. "Is tomorrow evening at seven o'clock all right?"

Aaron acknowledged that the time fit into his schedule as well and asked for their address and directions to their home. He arrived promptly the next evening with a large envelope. The greeting and introductions were graceful and cordial. Aaron was offered refreshment and invited to sit.

The home was well-maintained, everything in its place and a place for everything. In any decor Aaron was always drawn to portraits. His teaching repertoire had included a class in photography, and people were always his thing. Any other print was fine, but to him it was just stuff. There was a large picture in the entryway that included extended family, and a wedding photo graced the fireplace mantel. The sofa table held what appeared to be a son's graduation from college and a daughter's graduation from high school. The third picture was unmistakably Matthew in his military uniform.

JoAnne noticed Aaron admiring the photographs and gently stated, "God knows what it's like to let somebody graduate."

Aaron retrieved the envelope he had placed on the coffee table in front of him and began telling them about the week he spent as a substitute teacher for a speech class. He explained how everything was turned upside down, but in the end all the students had made decisions towards what they wanted to do with their lives.

Rick jumped in, "That was 'no words week.' Matthew told us about it. It was legendary. It's unusual that we didn't ask him more about his drawing. Maybe we assumed it was of the college he had chosen and attended for two years before he enlisted. We weren't shocked when he told us of his plans to serve. There had been traces of this throughout his life. We saw the change in him and didn't know whether his faith encouraged his decision to become a soldier or his decision encouraged his faith."

Aaron smiled and continued, "The class put together a 'No Words' book for me at the end of the year. They all included a representation of their decision. This sketch is from his senior year. Matthew believed with every fiber in him that this was ultimately what he was to do with the rest of his life."

The drawing was of multiple objects. Artistry was not Matthew's forte, but it was sketched well enough to determine what each object was. They all related to the soldier that he would become, the life in battle that he would choose. JoAnne and Rick were heartbroken when they received the news that Matthew had given his life.

JoAnne scanned and studied every pencil mark of every object on the sketch but lost her breath when she saw Matthew had included a chain necklace with a cross. They had given him a cross on a gold chain two years after this drawing, but it was not with the personal effects returned to them. She was just trying to continue with the evening when she said, "We have something to show you also."

They led Aaron down the hallway, past baby pictures where he couldn't help but linger. Matthew's room was at the end of the hall. Aaron found the room surprisingly inviting. A somber atmosphere would have been understandable, but it appeared JoAnne had found a balance between caring too much for the reminders that were left and not being able to face them at all.

She apologized that there was not more room to maneuver through Matthew's bedroom. "We know a lot of people leave rooms and memories untouched after a loss. We too didn't want to put anything away, but we didn't expect to be adding things at this pace. We've had lots of visitors who have reminisced and left symbols of their lives connected to Matthew's. He profoundly impacted our family. We didn't realize he had made so many lasting friendships, and we have heard from a number of people in his unit. We know every day mattered. Matthew's older brother has a family of his own now, and his children love to sleep in Daddy's old room. Our daughter in college frequently returns to her old room. It just made sense to have a place for Matthew's memories."

Aaron walked slowly around the room, investigating every photo and studying each memorial. He asked questions and spoke proudly of his former student. "Matthew just seemed saturated with good. Even though he was very young, he had a spirit of authority about him. He had a pure heart and was never empty when it came to his convictions. His faith was contagious."

JoAnne and Rick stood in the doorway and listened to this respected mentor speak so highly of their son. They watched him connect with various stages of Matthew's life and celebrate the people he blessed. Rick picked up a letter-sized envelope on the desk and handed it to Aaron. He opened it on their way back to the front room. It was obvious it had been opened and read many times.

Before reading any of it, he told them he knew of a letter Matthew had planned to write. Aaron hadn't personally seen it but understood why it was so precious to them. "Matthew came to see me after he enlisted, before he left for training. He stated that he was drawn to this mission even without knowing what it would entail. I affirmed to him that it would be difficult.

"He told me he intended to write a long letter containing his beliefs and ideals. He contacted me by phone during his training and as he was formulating his thoughts. As he began to write, everything in his life felt so significant. Matthew could predict with certainty that whether the letter was sent to you by his commanding officer or he returned and gifted it to someone who desperately needed hope, its purpose was far-reaching. He had been held captive by this mission."

Aaron couldn't miss the range of emotions Matthew's parents expressed as he told them about their time together. A sense of pride overwhelmed Aaron as he spoke. "I can attest to the change in Matthew. I knew the source of his strength and newfound purpose. Redemption and love captivated him and swept him off his feet. He was at peace with his decision and eager to start the mission. His devotion and concern for you fueled his commitment. Your love for him fueled his resolve."

"A father couldn't be prouder," Rick responded. "His testimony truly was a love story. Do you know his name means "reward"? He had time to consider the cost as well as the reward. I know he did not have this determination to help rescue the world in order to validate his own life. I didn't realize I could love him more until I read his letter."

Aaron still had not read any portion of the letter but felt it was the appropriate time to inquire about submitting Matthew's story to the museum. "I knew of the letter but wanted to be certain you were ready to release it. I also believe the next gift I ask of you is now appropriate.

"Staff at the museum have been asked to interview for one last biography. We're that close to capacity, and we will be holding a dedication ceremony soon. When the owner made the announcement that he'll be selecting from our list of final candidates, I immediately thought of Matthew."

There was no delay or uncertainty in Rick's voice as he answered. "We had heard the Jenski was getting pretty full and there was some sort of race to the finish. Because of this letter, when you contacted us about Matthew's story, we had already said yes. We treasure every word of the letter and now believe it is to be given to others rather than held so tightly by us. We have a copy for you to take with you."

Aaron chose to read it in their presence. He wanted to be able to ask and answer questions and allow them to elaborate wherever they felt appropriate, or simply because they needed to release their thoughts and emotions. He wanted them to be able to see the expression on his face as he celebrated Matthew's words and life.

He read the letter out loud. JoAnne and Rick had gone through each page countless times, together and individually, but felt they had not scratched the surface of its depth until this night when they heard for the first time the words read aloud. Aaron's voice did not remind them of Matthew, but it was a strong male voice, and it touched any remaining untouched fragments of their hearts. They had no idea there were any left.

Aaron recognized some of the concepts as he read the letter. Matthew had learned a great deal from him as his student. The message Aaron portrayed was powerful, and it came out clearly through Matthew's words.

The Letter

Mom and Dad, and anyone to whom this is given:

I've been thinking about being fearless probably since I was two years old. Then it was make-believe and pretend. I'm writing now before I deploy because I don't want to only hope to have time after deployment. This is too important. I have so much to tell you, and I feel like my head is full of too many words to get them all in this letter, but I will try.

Obviously I don't want you to receive the letter at all, but if you do, know that I found an undiscovered and noble part of myself in writing to you. Just knowing how you would have responded to me motivated me to complete it. I love you even more for that. Watching the two of you as I was growing up, I saw so many good things that I wanted to become. If this letter is to be experienced by others, you will know the appropriate timing.

I've not written a lot, and this is my first letter addressed to you. I believe this will help me work through my thoughts and clear my head and allow me to focus on my training. This writing provides a form of companionship, with you, with any potential reader, and with God. It forces an acceptance of reality and defies being beaten by that reality if it is unpleasant. It helps the writer and the reader heal.

More than all of that, I'm writing for something bigger than myself. I have a new love for purposeful words. I officially became involved when I had to place a notebook and pen beneath my bed and carry another set with me when permitted. I humbly asked God to not leave me alone or lonely until this letter was done. He must have experienced incredible companionship when He wrote the Bible.

I consider this a love letter to you and to God, to be used at His discretion. It has given me focus and sometimes taken it back, just as being in love often hijacks most of your attention. I did learn to put my thoughts on hold when required. Both the writing and the mission are inspired by my love for you and for people I haven't met yet, but mostly by God's love for me, and mine for Him.

If I could write this when all is well with the world, it would be easy, but all is not well with the world. In a sense, it must mean that this is something I'm not capable of on my own if it's not what I'm currently feeling in my heart.

I look forward to seeing the people overseas that we are helping. I am fascinated by a language and culture I don't understand. I am mesmerized, and someday I will speak that language. Someday all language will be one. Even misunderstandings will be nonexistent. Until then, God allows us to need each other to receive communication. I see this as an opportunity to bring people together. In an unusual way, it makes me feel connected to the world, a brief moment of being united with so many. I think that's the excitement of a stadium or arena.

There's also a lot of cultural language with the military. Dad, I know there are many industries that promote this tough language, and obviously in my youth I would not have been able to hold back my words, but now I feel liberated to speak only my faith. Between my spirit and my flesh, I want to show truth.

I have always wanted to be a soldier. Every stage of my life this desire has presented in a different form. I didn't exactly need to be taught how to play with guns and swords as a child. If you had not given me those things as toys, I would have found something to create them myself. Any cartoon with anything valiant was my favorite. As a teenager I was drawn to a war picture or film where justice triumphs. I have watched many patriotic ceremonies, solemn and victorious, and I have seen soldiers reunite and depart.

Every holiday we take time to remember those who sacrifice. My decision became clear and the timing felt right when I made a connection with what I have read many times, "This do in remembrance of Me." The concept of never forgetting the sacrifice took on new meaning. I began to see Jesus as the superhero. Every holiday turned into once upon a time there was Christmas and they all lived happily ever after because of Easter. I have always wanted to be a soldier. This just changed the reasons.

I know it may not seem logical for me to think this way, and I understand how this might encourage criticism. This isn't from a textbook, protocol, or guideline, but I've learned to listen to a source that is scholarly and unlike anything I've ever known. I have listened intently to the reverence in speaking of the

Beloved Soldier. It is all completely liberating. I would rather answer for my thoughts on earth to the creation than my disobedience in heaven to the Creator. I want to live without regret, knowing that I am accountable only to the One who calls my name at the rescue mission that counts.

This road is not for everyone, and those who come home injured or who do not come home at all do not diminish the sacrifice of those who come home safely. Every job requires sacrifice and service, and one calling is not elevated in its level of importance or sacrifice over another. I understand some people choose this employment because of responsibility to their family. I'm embracing this before having that responsibility to a family of my own, if that's the direction my life is to take.

Not just with work but also with life and relationships, every time I see a person put someone else's needs first, I will think of that verse, "This do in remembrance of Me." Everyone can have a medal of honor and enlist in a holy adventure. The motivation comes from love. It's the only thing powerful enough to redeem.

Don't get caught up in any conflict of information or controversy. The finest Soldier ever was subjected to conspiracy and cover-up, and His purpose and authority were questioned during regional power struggles. Those who spoke up for Him and knew the truth suffered for His good name.

I am unable to get my arms around world politics and underlying causes. I cannot submit to this mission for that reason only. I can, however, place my time on earth with the single entity who will not waste His resources or my willingness to serve. There is no abuse of power or lack of leadership under His direction.

When you see people exercising rights and freedoms that break your heart, please don't see it as taking advantage of our commitment. I believe in discharging my duty to God even and especially when something on this planet does not appear deserving. One soul is worth it all. Democracy, to me, is a picture of the freewill given to us by our Creator.

My picture of a military hero is Christ. If I had not experienced this love, it would seem strange. Even though it would draw me in, it's unfamiliar, so it would feel right to resist it because it must not be real. But I have experienced this love, and it is awesome. I have had so many opportunities to learn how far God's love reaches and what lingers to eternity. Look how many opportunities I have had to bring joy to my Father by responding in a way that isn't about this life, and look how many opportunities He has had to pour out grace when I have been too weak to see His love or respond accordingly.

Part of me is terrified, and part of me is in awe that God has chosen me in this way. It's my most favorite thing now, to be used as part of His design. It doesn't carry with it the negative connotation of being used by people. It's just a fraction of what Mary might have felt when she realized God had chosen her to carry forward His plan, but it's something we can all feel. We all carry Jesus to others. We're a human vessel planted with a talent or gift or truth or passion for something good, a part of who Jesus is to be carried to someone else through our life.

I wonder if the little boy with the fish and bread was one of those children who from a young age was destined to develop a nonprofit organization, or maybe he arrived as the rest of the multitude did with some issues to work through in their lives. He could have been awful by nature, but sitting on a hillside he was changed. How thrilling to be able to tell the story of what happened to him as God used his soft heart or came along and softened his heart, and fed a multitude. It took a small resource and an exercise of freewill. It makes sense to go to great lengths in order to raise funds and put together resources. We may be toiling and at the same time diminishing what God could have done with a small resource, a soft heart, and a yielding of freewill.

I'm grateful that you and others will pray for me. The easiest and most difficult prayer to give is, "not my will." There will be a constant whisper of voices recognizing God's authority. In the past I understood prayer only as "Dear God in the role of servant, here's what I want, or please clean up this mess." It's amazing to me that He loves both those roles, but He also has so many more. I used to feel guilty when I would pray because it was only when I needed something. I know He wanted me to ask, but now I realize there's so much more.

I wrongly believed that prayers needed to be sweat and tears for hours so I could earn the answer I wanted, or to the opposite extreme, they never required anything on my part. This part of my life has changed as well. I experience a prayer of love daily. Stories pull at my heart, even when I am supposed to be working instead of being caught up in a story, but stories are designed to pull at your heart. Sometimes they involve a huge loss or an awful event. It's more difficult if there are children in the story. It's more humbling if it involves someone who has harmed themselves or others. If I dig deep enough, there's a story behind that soul as well. That changes my perception from blame to truth and compassion. Prayer is as much for offense as defense, so I pray "Bless you, Lord. Love them through me."

Mom, don't worry. I know you have spent a lifetime packing extra thick socks in my bag, and double and triple checking that I have everything that I need. We go through an incredible amount of training here, but we cannot be prepared for everything in the real world, nor can anyone in civilian life. Sometimes basic things seem missing and sometimes extraordinary protections are provided. I could perish in a tank and survive without one. I have every weapon I need in the eternal war of good over evil, and I have the cross you and Dad gave me to remind me of that truth.

I don't know the definition of a life ended too soon. The design was that we never die, but redemption was provided when we did. The only thing I can pray is, "not my will." If this is awful for me personally but awesome for the kingdom, then I'm good with that. Nobody ever desires death and destruction, and nobody expects personal tragedy, but this time on earth is a blip compared to eternity. I'm sorry if it is to be a painful time.

As I look out the window, I see the beauty of death in the colors of fall. All the trees don't just turn colors one day, then lose their leaves and have their roots torn up and their trunks toppled to the ground the next. The colors linger, and there's even more beauty when they are all at different stages. Some are still green, and there are different shades of yellow, orange, red, purple, and brown. They're dying for the winter, a time to be dormant, only to find new life in another season, and the process has left scars even at their core, but growth from the outside.

If you are to grieve, be comforted that God parted with his Son knowing He would give His life. He has experienced the loss of a son. He knows the loss of a loved one. Look at what He went through to let us know His Son. I leave you with hard copies of words and pictures and soft copies of echoes and memories.

Love, Matthew

They sat in silence a few moments to collect themselves. JoAnne retrieved from the sofa table a small photo album that she had completed from the pictures referenced in the letter, and she showed it to Aaron. He studied each one and returned the book to her, then concluded the evening by telling them he would proudly submit the letter to his editor. He suggested the editor or the owner may have questions for them so he may be calling on them again. He mailed the copy of the letter as a formal introduction of Matthew to the museum. Nothing more would be needed. Who wouldn't want to have such purpose?

Journal

Colson

Colson was so excited to get to high school to explore the one thing he had always been interested in, but he was soon disappointed after investigating what was offered for photography. There was no longer a class he could take as an elective to obtain some of his credits doing something he loved, and there wasn't even an extracurricular club he could join.

He approached his advisor and inquired to see if there was anything that could be done. Colson was just a good kid, as they all are, and his advisor wanted to do everything possible to ensure that he could study what intrigued him. Colson's advisor knew the history of the photography class and called his former colleague, Aaron, to see if he could help.

In Garrick's former employment he owned a workshop with retail space in a strip mall. When he began his work with the museum, the owner assumed the expenses to maintain the shop. Since the associates would already be in the field, it made sense to preserve a site available for meetings, and they frankly needed the extra space for storage. The museum's priority had been more towards adding additional shelving rather than setting aside office space.

Aaron had been permitted to use some of the space to store remnants of supplies and equipment from his teaching days. When he got the call from his former colleague regarding the dilemma over the lack of a photography class elective, he was eager to dust off and brush up on his skills, and he made arrangements to meet Colson at the shop.

When Colson arrived, Aaron had already retrieved from the back room anything he had kept that could be used for their new endeavor, but he purposely left the unpacking, cleaning, and polishing undone to give the two of them something to do as they got acquainted. The afternoon felt like Christmas, discovering cherished decorations and ornaments and assembling electronics for optimum beauty and function.

They couldn't wait to get started on a couple projects they had schemed while organizing their recently unearthed treasures. They met once a week and often worked several hours. At times they would go to various locations together and photograph, and other times Colson would photograph on his own and they would use their shop time to process and collaborate on ideas. Their prints eventually covered nearly every available space in the shop, and they were easily viewed by passersby. Occasionally they would knock on the door and ask to take a closer look because they had been impressed by the quality and uniqueness.

For Colson, the lens provided so much more than pictures and images. It was a gift of vision to him. He could see how things used to be and should be and will be. Hours of discovery were afforded him because of his love for this craft. Colson often saw in the smallest creature the opportunity for something larger than life. He learned about life, and he learned about people. He watched others gain this insight through countless ways and knew how they felt. Hobbies and pastimes were opportunities to explore.

Every time he set up the telescope, he extended his view of the world. The binoculars taught him to see past the surface. He pretended to hold a set when he met someone new or was having a difficult time not judging by appearance. When he didn't focus, his perception of people was blurry, sometimes as if he was looking through the wrong side. This tool gave him insight and understanding and discernment beyond his years. Even a microscope represented to him the ability to see the impossible.

Aaron poured into him from his wide foundation on the subject, frequently mixing in his own take on how it related to life and the world around him. Colson soaked up everything Aaron poured. He learned the history of the cameras and understood how they worked and knew what lighting was appropriate and why. His hands were steady and his eyes keen.

Colson was a little late one day for their shop time. Aaron didn't need to read his mind. It was pretty clear he was angry. Aaron had been working on some framing when he showed up, so he put it aside and grabbed chairs for both of them. He had never seen him so upset and tried to assure him it would be good to get it off his chest. He was still hesitant until he looked up and caught Aaron's smile as he stated, "Spill it."

"No one ever wants to take the classes we have to take that Mr. Riley teaches. You can forget about the electives. He's like no teacher I've ever had before. I don't want my opinion of him to taint how I feel about all adults but especially you. Sometimes I wonder what must have happened to him that he's so full of evil. He is ruining lives, and he's trashing anything good that makes it more obvious that he is not."

Aaron calmly replied, "That's a start."

His anger turned to sadness as he continued. "He said you removed school property from the photo lab and lied about projects submitted by you which won awards. He claimed there were countless missing photos and anything good from your time here was because of your predecessor. He also said he has done nothing but clean up after you left and just can't believe students, parents, and the community as a whole think so highly of you."

Aaron had a response for every accusation leveled against him but knew Colson needed to work through it and asked, "Do you believe any of these things?"

"Well, no, but" -- he felt guilty for even thinking it. He had learned so much already from Aaron, and their time together was something he would draw strength from for the rest of his life. "It's just that I don't understand why you left. You have this old equipment, but the school doesn't even have some of these pieces. Some of the photos from the projects were dated before you worked for the school. I found some photographs here in school jackets. There is essentially no photography department there anymore. Why did you leave when you were so good at this and loved it so much?"

Aaron explained that what had been done was unforgivable, and the outcome would be far-reaching. "You are questioning the truth because of what you have been told. Mr. Riley knows the truth and chose to twist it. If we would study long and hard, we would discover his motivation, but it does not excuse his behavior.

"The photography instructor was teaching several seniors who had been with him all four years. They were doing incredible work and had multiple opportunities to submit their pieces for contests and presentations. He was so torn when he was offered a position that he had applied for years earlier, but the students were excited for him and encouraged him to go. Their team effort was even more impressive without a leader. Everyone involved was incredibly proud of what they were accomplishing. Most of the applications required the name of an adult supervisor who would be present when they were judged, so I stepped in."

Aaron laughed when he recalled what they did as they graduated. "They gifted me with their leftovers. The best pictures had been submitted in the contests, and they each kept a portfolio, but even these leftovers were excellent. I questioned whether they should be left to inspire future students but accepted them as a gift and memory of our time together. I did love my time there, and I am still teaching. I interact with a current student weekly, and I have conversations with former students and colleagues almost daily. Technically I'm still there.

"The students, parents, and community were simply appreciative that I was able to help complete the successes that had been building so long. There was a huge hole left after this class. It was like the school won the state title one year, and the next year the coach and the entire team were gone. I was substitute-teaching in many departments and was happy to have this assignment. The administration knew there would be great interest again someday and hired Mr. Riley with this department as one of his duties.

"Funding had been in place a year prior for new equipment, but the seniors wanted to finish their projects with the equipment they had used the previous three years. After they left, the administration asked if I had room to store the old equipment so they could make room for the new. Since I was the only one who had experience using it, they thought I might find a purpose for it someday. A year and a half later, we met at the shop.

"Mr. Riley diverted most of the funds to purchase backup equipment for his science lab. Staff did not understand how the order went through, but it was too late to change it. He defended his decision by stating there was more interest and money in science and everyone has a camera on their cell phone now anyway. We can investigate for a long time why he would do and say these things, but you're smart enough to figure it out or let it go."

Aaron reached across the table and put a firm hand on Colson's shoulder, looked him in the eye, and said, "Listen to me well. I'm going to recite something I heard a friend say to someone in a time of crisis. 'This happened for you, not to you.' Everything in life can be seen through that filter."

Colson was still processing through the drastic difference in what he had been told compared to what he now knew was true. He was not yet able to understand the concept from what Aaron had just said. It did calm his heart.

Aaron continued, "Someday you will have comrades so you can share ideas and experiences, but you will also be sharing a lab, equipment, and resources. Right now even though it is old, you have complete access to everything all the time. You will be able to appreciate and adapt to whatever tools you are given. You will have increased opportunities because of this humble beginning.

"You are free to have full control over the direction of your work, and no one will question what role you played in the project. Had I not left when I did, I could not have become your dedicated mentor, and I can't imagine not having this experience. Because you are not doing this for credit, you're not confined by grades. You're doing it because it is your gift. All teachers hope for their students a job that they would do even if they didn't have to in order to earn a living. Sometimes it's hard to understand at the time, but when you look back, you'll see the perfection in all of it."

Colson was determined to follow Aaron's example and be known for his integrity at the purest level. He was anxious to get back to work and asked Aaron if it would be all right if they shot no photographs that day but spent their time reviewing the collection of leftovers from the senior class he had helped. He wanted to be introduced to his comrades of the past, their personalities, talents, and techniques.

Since Colson was the entire photography department this year, the school newspaper staff asked him to take photographs for their sporting events. He was honored and thrilled to have a real assignment. He didn't want to fall into the trap of covering only the quarterback, the runningback and the receiver with the most stats, and the kicker, so he took a full-length candid picture of every single team member performing their distinct team function, including coaches, trainers, and managers.

Aaron was amazed and impressed with his tireless and inclusive approach to this responsibility, especially when he saw the sheer number of photos that covered every square inch available in their work area, but he couldn't help but jokingly ask, "And how do you plan to choose what will fit onto the one page you have been granted?"

Colson snickered, "Yeah, I know. I'm pretty sure this is over budget. Isn't it harder to put in all that team effort and then just sit on the bench?"

He did have a point. Aaron responded with enough insight to allow Colson to come up with a plan rather than being stuck over the issue of equity. "Perhaps because it is harder, it means more. It's actually a greater contribution. We are often asked to do something out of our realm. A player always wants to play a significant role to help the team. If that player is saying they want to score the winning point, there is probably an issue of pride there. They should be thinking more along the lines of relying on training and practice and maybe innate ability, then being faithful to the task. If called upon to score the last point, they accept the outcome, whether the hero or not.

"I really like your concept of team. I know any good leader would perpetuate that philosophy. With any challenge, like a limited budget and far more material than space, there is an answer that will conquer the desire to not let the limitations win."

Aaron knew Colson was not likely to give up on his ideals, so he gave him some space and time to think, while retrieving their dinner so they could work into the evening. Upon returning, he was delighted to see the solution that was offered. Everyone's full-length candid photo exhibiting their unique part of the team would be included, reduced to a size that they would all fit, laid out on a background of bleachers as a customary team photograph would appear, placed with no gaps and no overlaps.

Colson anticipated he would be asked if any of the individual shots would be large enough to recognize the identity, and he explained he intended to ask permission to display it on the large screen in the gym at the pep rally. He planned to use his one page in the newsletter to list every single name from the pictures he took and use the rest of this space to advertise team posters, which would be large enough to show identity and would be used to raise funds for a community service project, of course all of this pending approval.

The finished product was so popular that the students, school, and community requested a team poster be completed for each extracurricular organization in the district. Ultimately many nonprofit agencies benefited, and countless inspirational talks were given using these posters as a model of teamwork.

After such an accomplishment the previous week, it was perfectly acceptable the next to cut their time short to allow Colson to study for an exam. He did drop in at their agreed-upon time in order to let Aaron know about the exam and also to ask a philosophical question. That day in Economics, of all places, there had been some pretty intense conversation regarding some ethical considerations in one of their assigned pieces of literature. He was torn between what most of the class thought, what the instructor taught, and what he personally felt was right.

Aaron asked for the basics of the dilemma and then encouraged him to let it go while preparing for his test but pick it back up when he could devote some time to it, and they would talk about it the next week. His advice was figurative. "Write all over the pages. Take a red correcting pen to everything you believe doesn't fit or doesn't fit you. Question it. Search out your truth. Find a way to uncover what does fit you. It is only true freedom of speech if it is free of judgment. Share it with somebody you trust or reflect on it inwardly. The gift of being in someone's presence or just knowing how they would respond fuels personal development. You can choose to be who you are embellished by all the good qualities you have learned from those around you."

Since the subject was so vast, Aaron was sure there would be lots of opportunities for photographs as Colson was solidifying his opinion, but the next week he arrived at the shop with no photographs and a single piece of stationery with his point of view eloquently and strongly stated.

Aaron recalled that the topic at hand was value in the workplace. A lot of the classmates were looking forward to high-paying jobs since most were currently working for minimum wage. The teacher thought all things should benefit society as a whole. Colson optimistically believed everyone should earn the same wage and get to do what they love. Aaron appreciated the extraordinary effort put forth in arriving at his conviction.

"The problem is not our value but what we value and what has been valued all around us by society and family structure and deep within our soul. It's the biggest lie from the pit of hell. It causes us to do all kinds of things, sometimes wonderful and sometimes awful, to find the value we crave. It's mostly for the wrong reasons. We don't need to live with that load and suffer from its ripple effect that holds us back and then becomes a tsunami at a time of crisis if not settled.

"The founding father who so early on wrote 'All men are created equal' got it right. There is no favor of one person over another. All of life is validated. We have erroneously learned to place emphasis on the wrong things as defined by Harvard, Hollywood, the Hall of Fame, and Wall Street. The value is not in all of this stuff. It's only in what makes up your heart."

Aaron knew he had taken the assignment very seriously. They hadn't talked specifically about taking pictures to support his beliefs, but since it was such an automatic thing with Colson, Aaron asked him if he had been able to use his camera in formulating his thoughts. He replied, "I tried, but I saw a lot more inequality than I had hoped and couldn't bring myself to record it all."

The level of maturity was impressive. Aaron could see that Colson was approaching this topic from the same angle that formed his actions as he photographed the football team for the newsletter. He was aware that some of this was self-inspired, but when he acknowledged to Colson that some of it probably was also instilled by his parents, he noticed a tinge of resentment on his face and gently said, "I haven't met a perfect one yet."

Colson was still reflecting on the inequality he had seen. "What?"

"Parent, I haven't met a perfect parent yet."

Colson mimicked the sound his parents frequently made out of exasperation. "Parents are so" --

"Parental? Out of touch, misguided? I'm not even going to try to complete the list."

Colson fired back a sarcastic, "I know."

"Well, what are you going to do about it? You're the one with the forward thinking and plentiful creativity. You always see things in a different light when you look at it from behind the camera." They both understood that this would be the next assignment. It would be challenging, but beneficial.

The next week there were numerous photos to process, anything remotely resembling a parent-child relationship, all of which Colson took at the zoo. There was not one person included. Aaron had to admit that it was forward thinking and plenty creative. It was a great way to get around having to ask permission to photograph people in a setting depicting parenthood, and it did lighten the atmosphere and Colson's perceptions, so overall it was a successful endeavor. And it sure was fun processing them and drawing correlations to their human counterparts.

Aaron did feel the need to impart some amount of wisdom in the matter. He understood why any parent would be grateful for any time that a mentor spent with their son or daughter, and he believed it was a necessary gift for everyone. Colson received his advice with sincere appreciation.

"Don't let the fact that sometimes parents don't have time allow you to think nobody on earth has time for you. At times they sound disapproving, but it is actually worry they are feeling. They want to give you the world and all the knowledge to deal with it, but it's difficult to find and express the right words, and even if they do, sometimes you are not at a place to be able to receive them. They ache to have all the answers themselves and try to take advantage of every available opportunity to help, but now and then fall short with their methods. Every parent desires that their child be gifted with incredible, unending courage that completely envelops who they are."

Since his last idea went over so well, Colson thought he would take the opportunity to share his latest solution for ending what ails society. "Hey, I have another really great idea."

"What's that?"

"I noticed Sunday the school looked pretty lonely, but the churches were happy and full. Then all week long the schools are bustling and the churches are sad and empty, except Wednesday night. I believe the schools are supposed to schedule lightly on a Wednesday for that reason. They meet at opposite times, and they both need classrooms, a kitchen, a gym, and an auditorium. Wouldn't their budgets go a lot further if they worked together?"

Aaron was again amused by his forward thinking. "That's an excellent idea, but then there's that whole church and state thing."

"Yeah, but weren't those the same people that were smart enough to say we were created equally? Intelligently compassionate but not practical, I guess."

"Wouldn't hurt the churches to have the opportunity to work with the community and its leaders."

"Wouldn't hurt to have a few prayers of protection linger in the school halls."

"Too many denominations to get together."

"But there's supposed to be only one church."

The banter was constant. It was Aaron's turn. "Churches could do more and give more."

"Schools could cancel fees and still have enough supplies."

"They could fund-raise together!"

"They would probably argue over who used up the remaining sporks, you know, a spoon and a fork, one utensil to save money."

70

"They would probably argue over their share of the water bill."

"Yeah, you'd have to install a flush meter that recorded a date and time."

The conversation was getting a little overboard, so Aaron asked a reasonable yet thought-provoking question. "Aren't those debate team members at your school usually also a part of the student council?"

The back-and-forth had been so quick that Colson responded with a simple "yes" and then realized where this was going after the short pause. "Oh, right, and they generally frequent board, commission, and city council meetings to learn the ropes."

"Probably apply for internships at various levels as well."

"Maybe someday even run for office."

The two comrades gave each other a fist bump in affirmation and celebration of their magnificent idea. They were dangerously brilliant together.

The next week, Aaron was prepared to ask Colson to consider being a part of the museum. As light as the previous week had been, he expected a little trepidation with his request on this day, but he also knew how impactful this opportunity could be for him if chosen.

Colson arrived with more photographs to process. Except for his work with the school teams and organizations, he seemed to be more interested in photographing objects rather than people. He had discovered early on how differently people behave when placed in front of a camera. Part of it was fun and uplifting, but sometimes it seemed a little over the top to him. If he did photograph people, he took unposed shots with permission. He learned more of their true character this way.

All of that time spent looking into the lens at objects and people helped him see himself as well, but he also realized how difficult that had been for him. It was easier to look outward. Of course it was a difficult time in his life, as he was often reminded, you know, all that stuff about being between a child and a man.

Aaron had talked to him before about the work with the Jenski Museum but had not explained the details of his own latest assignment. All of Colson's excitement and questions were related to the art gallery. When Aaron shared the information about the last biography and asked if he could submit his story, Colson didn't quite know what to think and responded, "We still have so much work to do."

His answer confirmed to Aaron that he was wrestling with far more than their shop time and portfolio. He assured him they would continue with their weekly efforts. He also realized the notion of having to, in a sense, be in the picture rather than taking it was intimidating to Colson. The biography camera would be the broadest form of eye contact there is, and to make eye contact with that camera would no doubt feel like any viewer would be able to press the zoom button to his soul.

Aaron radiated certainty when he told him, "I've always been more than okay with exactly where you are, which I'm sure makes it seem confusing when I'm so excited with the progress as well. You don't have to wait until your portfolio is finished before sending what you have completed to the gallery, and you don't have to wait until your story is finished before sending who you are already to the museum."

The thought of incomplete work did not set well with Colson. He had always heard that you are to finish what you start, and that was just his nature anyway. He might be able to get past this with his photography if he could somehow mark "partial" on its cover, but even "work in progress" on a possible book wouldn't comfort him. He confided, "Understanding photography has been easier than understanding myself. How do I possibly figure myself out enough to be a book?"

Aaron's words alleviated his fears. "We'll help you with that. Photography is a big part of who you are, but it is only a small part of who you really are. You are more about the book than the photos, but if displaying your work in the museum helps us see your soul, it's a wise tool. Be as inclusive with yourself as you are with others. There's always more to learn, when you are ready. It's never too much or too soon."

With that kind of confidence shown to him, Colson could genuinely respond, "Who wouldn't want to be unveiled in that gallery?" He wondered what he ever could have done to deserve the hours Aaron spent pouring into his life and found himself wanting to do the same for others. Over and over he would draw from the analogies slipped into his heart as he was studying this craft.

The view to the world was his to explore. In his own way, as with each individual, he would be all right. Each pass of the lens magnified his destination. Sometimes it would require a flash, but the tools were there and capable of the task.

Aaron sent to his editor photographs along with this application, and then he added more than a few pages to his journal concerning Colson because of their many interactions together.

Journal

Intermission

G arrick sent out invitations to the team for a dinner party of sorts. It was really just an excuse to get everyone together, because it seemed like infinity had passed between now and when they parted. It was not that he was impatient. He just loved their camaraderie, and he was eager to meet the candidates, so for now he could listen to Kecia and Aaron detail these potential biographies and watch them light up the room with their expressions of pride. He had thought to schedule the evening in town at a special restaurant, but he knew Kecia and Aaron probably felt as fondly towards the museum as he did towards his time in the field. He had connections with some really good caterers, so the invite was to the Jenski conference room. He was thankful the shelf with the one missing book was located in this room. It was the focal point of their social event.

Jaimin was happy to oblige Garrick's initiative, and even happier to see his staff. Each had submitted two applications, and Garrick and Jaimin had reviewed and discussed them at length, but this was an excellent way to take care of any details now to avoid delays later, when the focus would be the approaching dedication ceremony. This also brought Jaimin and Garrick closer to the story, something they appreciated profoundly.

After dinner and conversation they once again toured the museum in its nearly finished state. They reviewed some of the archives to try to comprehend what it would feel like to place the last one on the shelf. They all knew that moment would be indescribable. Kecia and Aaron had three more applications to submit, and Jaimin had an extraordinary event to prepare. Garrick thanked them all for accommodating his exuberance and said he would happily return to his office, only for a short time.

Journal

Rhesa

Rhesa telephoned her mother but was so upset she could barely speak. All the usual fears entered her mother's thoughts as she heard her daughter weeping. Someone had died or had been in an accident, or perhaps she had lost her employment. When her mother slowly began to understand the words through the tears, she was heartbroken and in disbelief. The wedding that they had looked forward to and planned for many months now was canceled. She adored Rhesa's fiancé and believed they made a great couple. Everything seemed to be going well, so what possibly could have happened?

A large part of the unsettling nature of the sudden breakup was that there seemed to be no reason for it. Rhesa's fiancé stated that it was because of her unrealistic dedication to her job, the long hours and lack of time for him, but this had been her practice since the two met three years ago.

She had studied and prepared for a position in personnel but was unhappy with her current job because it seemed to be 90% administration, 10% people. The people she worked with were lovely, and her employer was almost overly appreciative of her efforts. She just didn't have much direct contact with them.

Spending such a large part of her day with this discontent caused her to put in even more time to try to find some fulfillment in her chosen career. Her unhappiness crept into her activities outside of work and ultimately her relationships, so when her plans to marry and start a family were destroyed when her fiancé broke their engagement, it was a loss of not only a significant part of her life but the only thing she had left.

She wanted a marriage and family and thought she was working hard now in order to be able to devote more time to her real dreams later. Maybe the reality of a lifetime of her being married to her job and his lack of hope for change really was his breaking point, but she believed that there was more to it than that and that she probably would never really know or understand.

She would have the weekend to get herself together and then head off to work Monday morning attempting to move forward as though she was fine and nothing major had happened, but by mid-morning Monday she found herself in her employer's office by his request. When she began to explain what had happened, he promptly suggested that she needed to take some time away from her employment. She resisted and told him she needed her work in order to remain occupied.

He gently told her that her decisions and productivity had been suffering recently, he believed because of her lack of time away. He reminded her of all the times that she had readily stepped in when others needed or wanted an extended break, and now it was her turn. He insisted. When he suggested a month, he might as well have cut off her leg. Whatever would she do without this crutch? She could think of worse addictions that she could have become consumed with to absorb her time and thoughts, or maybe not.

Rhesa had spent time with her mother over the weekend to try to come to grips with her new reality. Her mother tried to console and advise her but felt her attempts were inadequate and perceived herself as almost too motherly, desiring to be the mama bear defending her young, which really wouldn't help Rhesa process realistically. She feared they would spend the sabbatical month with chocolate and sad movies and do more harm than good, and she would be no more prepared to go on with life after a time of such little healing than she was in her current state.

She also had watched her daughter endeavor to support a friend through a divorce and then try to recover after the heartache when that friend ultimately took her own life out of despair. Rhesa was angry with her friend at the time and was not even now in such a desperate place herself but had more understanding concerning why her friend felt so despondent. She regretted terribly not being able to say or do the right things at the time to help. Because of the enormity of hopelessness she felt with her own loss, she couldn't grasp how anyone is ever able to withstand the emotional turmoil of divorce.

Rhesa's mother wanted to provide more help than she could personally give, and she wasn't even slightly aware of what approach she should take, so she called her friend, Kecia, and asked if Rhesa might be able to stay with her a few days. Kecia had been supportive during a difficult time in her own life, and she hoped for the same experience for her daughter.

Rhesa was at ease with the arrangement because she had already met Kecia on a couple of occasions, so she didn't feel like a complete social case. The two talked through some things Rhesa had not been able to make much progress with during the conversations with her mother. She prided herself on being low maintenance and believed there were far worse problems in the world than hers, but every part of her felt like it ached from the inside out.

Kecia told her that her concerns for the entire world could wait. "As things go wrong with parts of our lives, we search for greater meaning; we branch out. We get pruned and we blossom. What you are looking for is within you."

She noticed Rhesa's tendencies toward perfectionism and playfully suggested that she intentionally submit herself to something completely imperfect. "Perfectionism is the opposite of unconditional love. We laugh and sometimes are proud of this trait, but it's a trap that pushes us to give more of ourselves than we should to something that will never be perfect. And it expects the same from others. Any over-achieving personality will have a tendency to give too much. What in this life is more important than your soul? If anything is done to prove ourselves, including trying to be perfect, it is not the right motive and it is not necessary."

Rhesa acknowledged that she reveled in the pursuit of perfection and often wouldn't want to be involved at all if perfection wasn't possible. She supposed she had missed out on lots of opportunities. She understood that the question Kecia next put forward was asked out of love.

"Is that sometimes true also with some of your relationships?"

The sigh that was returned after a pause could have been of grief or anger, but it instead signified relief. It was far too early for closure, but just knowing part of her mistake gave her comfort and hope that she could learn from this truth and apply it to many areas of her life.

Kecia continued, "We all are flawed. Perfect love is possible only with your faith."

Rhesa admitted she had probably put too much stock in all the fairy tales society portrays at all stages of life. "Even when I don't read and listen to and watch that stuff, I'm discontent." Kecia was disgusted, but not with Rhesa. "You're too smart to fill your head with that noise. You need time without the clutter to listen to nothing but the wind and understand how rich your life is."

It was evident that what Rhesa really needed now was seclusion, which seemed unusual given the fact that a huge part of what she felt was loneliness. She lived alone, but she was always working or socially committed, so she didn't really have an opportunity for solitude.

Kecia had lots of contacts and knew of a friend's place where Rhesa could stay. His cottage wasn't lavish, but it was just a few minutes' drive to the ocean. He was actually out of the country, and Kecia was certain he would appreciate having someone reside there for a while and care for it so that it didn't appear so desolate.

Indeed he was grateful to hear from his friend and explained that he was unable personally to stay at his place because of time constraints, so he was pleased to have a temporary resident and graciously granted her permission to use the cottage as long as she desired. He gave her contact information for the person in town who kept his accounts in order and his key in a safe place, and he said that he would let that individual know to expect Rhesa. If she had any questions, she could contact the same person. He insisted to Kecia he required no compensation.

The cottage was unique, rustic, and comfortable. More importantly, it was secluded. There was no television, perfect to dispense with any temptation to live in someone else's world anyway. It was also a few minutes to the nearest town, which would keep her from spending too much time shopping and sightseeing.

For this respite to be all that it was supposed to be, she realized a lot of her time needed to be a concentrated effort towards doing nothing, but even that would take a while to master. She needed to do something with her mind other than reflect on how she arrived at this place in her life and what she could possibly do about it.

Her first evening, she inserted a CD she had found while unpacking and set the music at low volume and continuous play. She settled in on the couch with a blanket and a substantial-sized book and fell asleep while reading. No alarm sounded at 5:00 a.m., and she awoke feeling better than she had in weeks. The temptation was resisted to plow through a customary morning routine, but there wasn't a lot of the morning unspent anyway.

In her box of something-or-other with preservative, enough food remained to suffice for her first meal, but this would be her last processed dining experience here. With the nearest food source more than a vending machine away, there would actually have to be meal planning and some real cooking, and she promised herself she would make things from scratch, fresh, no frozen entrées. She upped the challenge when she unplugged the microwave just to see if she could survive. Hardcore campers who have slept under the stars would still think she was a lightweight, but to her this was roughing it.

With her long days at the job, cooking like this would have been an incredible waste of time, and eating was an interruption she only put up with because it was required. Now even this mundane part of life became a journey in self-discovery. The reading she brought did not include one cookbook, but when she found what was obviously a treasure of favorites compiled by what she envisioned was a local ladies society of blue ribbon winners from the county fair, well, it would be unthinkable to not try a new recipe daily.

A visit to the ocean was a necessity on the first full day of scheduled tranquility, and the optimum time for the smallest crowd on this day was during the evening, so the plan was to grocery shop in the afternoon and sink her toes in the sand at sunset, unless that too closely resembled an agenda.

She had been in the work cave too long, and it was almost embarrassing to be so completely delighted in public with something as trivial as the many and various colors of fresh vegetables. For the amount of time she spent shopping for groceries, her purchases were not many, and she several times had to return to the shelf an item that formerly jumped into her cart automatically. But it was a start.

As conscious as she was of the people around her as she shopped, it was beyond understanding how she felt she had the entire beach and vast ocean to herself, and yet was not lonely. Rhesa sat and looked deep into the tide and wondered where the starting point was and how long it took to reach this side. She asked of herself to be mentally, emotionally, and spiritually pliable and agile every day of this quest in her transformation. She affirmed that it would not be soon enough when her heart would be new, but she would be at peace while she waited.

The next day she planned nothing so she could, as Kecia suggested, listen to nothing but the wind. She heard every time the wind moved the air and every time the wind moved anything and every time anything moved in the wind. She watched and listened to its essence a good part of the day. It was far better than anything else she had previously done to dissolve her time. It was unforced and unforeseen. Each element was distinct yet harmonious, and she felt as though it was planned uniquely just for her, like a date. Each sudden shift in the view provided confirmation, and each subtle change served to deepen the message. Wildlife arrives with no fences to place it or contain it there.

Her next trip to town would demand she find an art store, even a toy store if that was all that was available to acquire the paint supplies necessary to capture the land and seascapes as she witnessed them. She had not painted in years and had forgotten the inspiration she received from it. Her talent was not exceptional, but the experience for her was almost like a prayer.

The following day while in town, Rhesa found an area that seemed almost designed for studying humanity, so she purchased a cappuccino and retrieved a book from her vehicle. She was sure to learn something about herself and life's mysteries as well. She watched as people went to great lengths to be a part of something or to appear significant. Some people looked lonely even in a pair or group, and it almost magnified their expressions to be both together and alone. Others who were alone did not look lonely.

She noticed the demands women placed on themselves and society and wondered if men had even close to the same makeup. Why do women have a need to be the most important thing in the world to somebody, everybody? If one person or attribute rejects or eludes them, it may as well be the whole world. Substance and feelings should influence appearance, not the other way around. Everything seemed to be no deeper than the surface. Women responded to life based on their appearance and men responded based on their pocketbook, from their own definition of beauty and wealth. People do act differently in a public arena, but it was still a gloomy realization. She concluded that people are vastly different and altogether similar, and loneliness is more a state of mind than a result of circumstances.

Every day something entirely unexpected happened. At her employment, that would have meant an extra load or something broken that she was required to fix. All tasks now to her intimated something much deeper. As she cooked and painted and as she cared for what would be her home for just this one month, she compared every ingredient and instruction, every angle and scene, every accommodation and accessory to something larger than life, and her pliable and agile heart changed.

This undertaking wasn't just learning something new but dispensing with the old first. It required an inordinate amount of attention and sometimes took the attention from a more pressing matter. Remarkable repetition was essential and intense motive imperative. At times transformation happened with ease because it was not so in conflict with previous perception and sound logic, but it still felt like learning to walk all over again. Other times growth was necessarily helped along only by remembering trusted words of advice. Still other times it was such a difficult concept that no amount of knowledge or practice or even encouragement broke the barrier. It was out of her hands.

The temptation was there to avoid the effort or to become impatient. It helped that she was attempting to make sweeping changes all at the same time to dispense with any stray related rationalizations so she could approach an old situation confident in her new and comprehensive mindset. It also helped to find the easiest way possible to accomplish such a goal. At some point it became more comfortable. She once again affirmed that it would not be soon enough when her heart would be new, but she would continually be at peace while she waited.

Kecia had left instructions with Rhesa to get in touch with her if she wanted to visit together at the cottage, but otherwise she would be on her own. Her only assignment, learn to love herself; that's it. It had been three weeks, and she was ready and wanting to speak with Kecia. Rhesa didn't want the month to end, and yet she was ready to return to her life yesterday.

When Kecia arrived, she was greeted with sun tea and lemon bars straight out of the blue ribbon book. As she hugged

Rhesa, she caught a glimpse of a series of paintings on a bookcase and remarked about their intricacy. Even more noticeable was the change in her spirit. Part of the result of all this for Rhesa was a new definition of love. All she could do was display it because she sure couldn't explain it.

The two chose to sit on the porch and catch up on the events of the past three weeks. Kecia said that Rhesa's employer had recently called her mother. "He was just checking in, and he said to take all the time you need. He also said that he realized he was partly responsible for this as well, and he missed the dedicated and capable employee he used to have before he worked her too hard. He thought you were handling it well and actually seemed to thrive on the experience. He knows now to be more guarded and not to put you in that position. He said he would rather have his help take short enjoyable breaks than need extended ones out of desperation."

Rhesa expressed her appreciation for the delivery of the message and acknowledged its truth. Before meeting Kecia, for such a long time Rhesa felt nothing but alone. She now felt a part of something she still didn't fully understand, but it was encouraging, respectful, comforting, and fruitful. She told Kecia she didn't need more time; she was ready. "I'm able to get my arms around something more than just an existence.

"This time of stillness has allowed me to redefine who I am at the core. After being away, I look forward to providing for details personally and professionally that I otherwise might not have cared about. I know many parts of our lives go through this same cutting away and restoration. Some things will still be difficult, but there's a new joy in some things that used to be unnoticed or mundane, and it's an honor to care for all of it.

"It's the mountain after the valley, the rainbow after the storm, the oasis after the desert. I know it's only been a short time of healing and there will be more valleys and storms and deserts, but they are dependent on each other. The mountain was always preferable, but now my tears are of gratitude. Instead of wanting more strength and wisdom and provision, I just want more love, to give. "

When Rhesa announced the direction of her future with such confidence, Kecia understood the encounter she had had. Rhesa could discern the path. Her view had changed. She felt she had been given clear insight. Until now she had only been able to see a small area directly where she was. This process gave her farsightedness.

Kecia believed Rhesa surprisingly might be ready to consider an invitation to enter her story with the museum. She explained to her the details and said she understood if she was not prepared yet for such a monumental step. When her initial response appeared to be the often expected "why me," Kecia inquired if she was struggling with the concept of kings and queens, nobles and knights. When Rhesa grinned as though her mind had been read, Kecia replied, "They are all love stories in one form or another. You've been asked to participate for a reason."

Kecia was very persuasive, but she truly won Rhesa over to the idea when she said, "With the writing and editing, how could this story not have merit? Not to mention the facilities and resources and business model and countless hours from the dedicated team members. A love story makes everyone ache. We are designed to long for happily ever after. You've been blessed, and your perception is good. This will remain with you. You don't have to look to other sources. This is your place of rest."

Rhesa responded that she believed she was ready to share her story if selected. She felt strong enough to reach out to others who were suffering. It had been long enough. She could now grieve with them and help them find a harvest in the embers that would only make them stronger and validate the purpose of it all.

Kecia encouraged her to deal often through the day with any confusion that she felt. "Keep yourself porous and tender. The things we can't settle when we are awake, I believe we are granted in dreams."

Before Kecia left that evening, Rhesa retrieved from the top of the bookcase one of her paintings and presented it to her. She had specifically thought of her while working on it. Kecia thought to include the painting with the information she forwarded to the editor but couldn't possibly when she saw how perfect it looked on her own bookcase.

Rhesa took a couple days to wrap things up at the cottage and try to wrap up her experience as well. She did want to stay forever and compared her life to a long car ride on the way to a dream vacation. She would keep busy with activities and stops along the way to pass the time and make the trip not seem so long. She expected joys in the journey, and heartaches, but the goal is the destination. This place would serve to remind her of that when she became weary.

She cleaned and organized and rearranged some accessories she had purchased in town to show how grateful she was for this opportunity. It appeared as though it had been some time since anyone else had been able to stay. She was delighted to embellish this place with which she fell in love. Anything she added was easily subtracted, and the painting she placed on the counter was her version of a thank you card. She packed the remaining two paintings for her mother and herself.

Her last evening, she took a cappuccino, some caramels, and her favorite book to the ocean. Her blanket was close enough to briefly allow the water to reach her feet. She lit a candle and played soft music so she could hear the waves in the background. She listened to and felt the wind and watched the water glisten and appreciated the enchantment of the wildlife.

She returned the key a different person.

Who wouldn't want this love?

Journal

Ragan

Ragan and Kecia had been friends for most of their lives and in recent years faithfully once every other week went out in the evening to dinner, always the same place, usually the same food, which was only eaten as one came up for air to give the other the opportunity to participate in all the catching up needed. It was as though they hadn't seen each other for two years. It was almost to the point where the standard meal choice was on the counter at 6:00, and it was a given that they were the last to leave before the doors locked.

They met when Ragan was only five years old, and they went through life together. Kecia was older, and Ragan looked up to her and admired her. At their biweekly dinners they bounced back and forth ideals and points of view, and the more they learned together, the hungrier they became to explore the next question.

Nobody showed up with a piece of paper stating the topic of the evening. The other would have laughed loud enough to disrupt the dinner hour. They wouldn't have stuck to it anyway. Occasionally an article or text would be used to throw down the challenge, but it was certainly not needed for fear of dead air.

Ragan's understanding of people and the intricacies of life grew every time she listened to Kecia. Her ability to perceive beyond the obvious and ordinary matured as they spent time together exploring every topic important to them. Some of the best advice Ragan received was to allow herself to be frail.

She was now at a time in her life where the more she discovered, the less she seemed to understand its meaning. She was thankful for their friendship in part because she was certain Kecia must have walked others through this obstacle course because of her gift in balanced conversation.

If asked at any given time where she was with her uncertainties, Ragan would describe herself as distracted, but still in a better place than she had been previously when she felt overtaken with fear and doubt. She had checked what society deemed to be standard expert advice against what she knew to be true and wondered, if it was expert, why the results looked as they did. Invariably in these situations intuition told her that the only thing expert about standard societal advice was its packaging.

She often needed to think out loud and recruit help in her search to find resolution over complex and crucial philosophies. She tried to listen to the right people, without being consumed by her pursuit of something substantive and sincere. When she felt empty, Ragan remembered Kecia telling her that her faith was the source of constant, overflowing life.

Listening to Kecia talk about principles caused Ragan to be in a place where she had never been. It was this strange mix of being a child learning for the first time and soaking it all in to a maturity level well beyond yesterday. Ragan could spend the whole evening with her and not hear one critical, judgmental remark. When she asked her how she had acquired this skill, Kecia responded, "The best of us is judged. The rest don't need to be."

With that level of mental latitude, it would be very manageable to be on board with nearly anything Kecia proposed.

Ragan loved to hear her talk about her work with the Jenski Museum. She knew there was a special project coming up and couldn't wait to hear the details, but when Kecia sat across the table and asked her personally to participate, her immediate and firm reply was simply, "Good grief."

Of course it would be easy for Kecia to win interviewer of the year with the amount of background info she had on this one, but that's not why she asked her to consider taking part. All the unresolved questions still after all these years would undoubtedly get second and third looks and make for invaluable stirring of future readers.

Their relationship had a strong foundation, and they continued to spend time together, but it was only because of the great amount of love and trust Ragan held for her that she was open at all to the concept. "I know my relationship with God is all I've ever needed, and then He blessed me with an awesome family like an undeserved and extravagant Christmas bonus. If there's anything within me in addition to all of that, I question whether it is enough for an entire book. I'm not some expert people should turn to for wisdom. What do I have to offer to fill even a chapter? There are still too many unanswered questions."

Kecia replied, "It doesn't matter, if it's for the right reason. The outcome is actually positive. It will be obvious who's on your side. There are things you should question. A lot of people try to claim something is virtuous when it's their own agenda they are trying to promote. Bottom line, it shouldn't conflict with your faith, but there's a destructive mindset out there that I believe will get worse. That's all in the past for you. You have something greater now. It's substance over fluff, certainty over fallacy."

Ragan was apprehensive that her thinking would be misconstrued. Anyone who had been frequently misunderstood would know what she was talking about. It was not that she didn't understand how everyone is unquestionably distinct, but some of her thinking was just out there. Her divergence used to terrify her, and then she went through this rebellious embracing of being contrary, and then she experienced a content acceptance and appreciation of the difference.

If she was able to ultimately attain a level of comfort in expressing her point of view, there was then also dilemma with appropriately choosing her words. She had spent a considerable amount of time practicing her communication skills but was often frustrated that the occasion to express herself and the words to do so did not show up at the same time. She sensed this was redeemable with a possible opportunity to put both to paper.

When Kecia asked her to be involved in this endeavor, she knew Ragan would need all of the next two weeks before their next get-together to be prepared to give her an answer. That's just the way she was, in part because she took everything so seriously, and also because she required a lot of patience.

Kecia told her to reflect on her thoughts and circumstances and they would talk about it at their next dinner, and then she encouraged her friend to consider the positive impact this could have. "If you think something, that's all well and good. If you know it, you will reflect it more often. If you talk about it, you hold yourself to task. If you offer it, you become it."

In making her decision, she thought back on many of their question and answer sessions. She knew Kecia did not intend for her to lose sleep over this, but again, that's just the way she was. The only thing she was secure in was her relationship with God, and that did not take place because of her efforts. She felt lost and found, and lost, and found.

He many times had parted the sea, and still she wondered if tomorrow He would allow her to traverse a mud puddle. At times she saw His guidance even in advance of the evidence, sometimes she was able to witness it directly, but far too often it was only after every element of her impasse fell into proper alignment that she acknowledged His loving authority. And yet He did not push, nor did He pull in various confusing directions. He simply led.

Ragan and Kecia had known each other for years before they began getting together every other week. They had contacted each other often for support or for an event and also to share news or a grand idea. They both understood what a gift it was to have this mentoring relationship.

For Ragan it was a time of searching. Her primary concern was for her children, or maybe herself as a parent. It was truly what brought her to her knees and also the one area where she desperately wanted to excel. She did possess maternal skills but believed her children deserved a genius, as does every parent.

She listened to Kecia talk about allowing herself to be taken off the parental pedestal so that it didn't limit a child's perception to human flaws. She appreciated the advice to acknowledge weakness knowing that God picks up after all his children, even when they have children of their own. Though we now grasp as an adult the great lengths our parents went to for us when we were children, we can only begin to grasp what God has always done and will always do even when we are not aware.

The discussion helped to renew Ragan's hope for the grace she would need to be faithful for the gifts granted to her care, and also for the selective memory she desired in order to recall only the favorable moments raising children, as God does with us. She wanted to approach each day with dedication, remembering the joy of their birth and looking forward to the pride in their development. This stuff in the middle is where she needed help. She was too overwhelmed to speak her prayer that night, and in that moment felt closer to knowing the love God must have for us.

Ragan continued to reminisce. One evening the conversation was particularly theological. They covered adoption and abduction, freewill, eternity, and why bad things happen to good people. She didn't want to become hung up on peripheral issues when to her there was only one important component to faith. The rest was not about the argument or the difference of opinion but the longing for a deeper relationship that she found exhilarating. It was bothersome that centrality was frequently not enough to avoid discourse and pain among people with more than sufficient reason for unity.

Since Ragan believed that every answer is contained in Scripture, they filtered these topics through its pages, and she wondered why the world's experts didn't tap into this inexpensive and expeditious resource to solve every problem known to man. She was also curious about what life would have been like before the Bible existed. Kecia believed that ministers conveyed the message to those who needed it.

Ragan saw a deep connection between physical and spiritual adoption and physical and spiritual abduction and noted as well that they are rival opposites, parenting by choice and protecting at all costs against abuse, trafficking, and murder, versus stealing someone else's child and fulfilling self-interests. Physically and spiritually, we are all deserving of adoption and vulnerable to abduction, but sometimes we rebel against a parent and aid a perpetrator and then require a rescue effort to be set in motion.

It wasn't the choice of topic but the choice of human behavior that caused Kecia to be so visibly bothered. Ragan was also upset having learned about a new medical procedure parents can undergo to assure the gender of their child. She wondered what it does to a child's self-identity if they unknowingly believe their whole life they were supposed to be somebody completely different. We can't pick their hair and eye color and facial features and build, nor can we pick their personalities, health status, choice of hobby or career, and we certainly can't pick their relationships. We get to unconditionally love the child that we are given, and God shows us how perfect His plans are in all areas of our lives. If God gives us freewill, He set the ultimate example of unconditional love.

Ragan stated that sometimes she would like to be able to give back her freewill and that it was perplexing that God would give to us something so dangerous but necessary. He knew how we would abuse it, but it was more important to Him that we not be inanimate objects to be placed on shelves and admired, incapable of serving any purpose. It was more important to Him that we be able to communicate and love, that we be real and not plastic. He had the whole universe, and yet He craved relationship and created us with the same desire for real love.

They could barely close one topic before opening another. As a child Ragan used to try to figure out eternity, to understand the concept of something never really ending in contrast to a world with an awful lot of boundaries. It was too big of a stretch. As an adult it would be difficult to think the opposite, an ending to something so wonderful or God having limited abilities. The only problem with eternity is waiting for it, and perhaps being at peace with the world in its current state in the interim. And God is patient. The planet appears to be on tilt. He responds with sufficient grace.

Ragan understood that destruction did not originate with God and knew He could bring a halt to anything at any moment, so the only way she could accept what she observed was to believe His focus is eternal reward over temporary circumstances. He knows the alternative. He is more concerned about the status of our soul in eternity than our status in this life. He intended for us to have both. We chose. She was grateful that Adam took the fall because if he hadn't put Eve before God, Ragan was convinced she would have found something to put before Him on her own anyway.

As philosophical as that evening had been, the next one she thought back on was simply honest. They talked about addictions. Kecia often let Ragan answer her own questions, knowing it would solidify her beliefs. She also would challenge her if she didn't feel Ragan was tracking with an appropriate response. A good friend does that, even when it makes the discussion difficult.

It didn't matter what the addiction was; Ragan put all of them in the same classification of attempting to feed our soul with something that was never designed to satisfy it. There were only two categories, in her mind, behavioral, which included addictions to relationships, hobbies, wealth and health, or the lack thereof; and substance, which could technically be considered behavioral as well.

She wondered why God created us so physically and emotionally hungry, thus leading to the substance and behavioral addictions. She believed both hungers were intended to be supplied spiritually, constantly. It was the only way to explain a loving God and a world so full of physical and emotional hunger, and she was angry that any of it was glamorized. If she focused on the truth, she could let things go that are harmful yet somehow are also compelling. A lie evokes this emotion, and evil can be alluring still when good is right next to it. It's debilitating. When reality wins, restrictions aren't necessary.

When Kecia said with confidence that everything wrong hinges on lack of faith, her words pierced Ragan. How could she establish so much in such a non-condemning way? Ragan was mesmerized listening to her pray and found her own prayers transformed in her presence. She was humbled to know how often she had been embraced in those prayers. She recognized the miracle of the darkness that was gone after one of the most intense evenings she and Kecia had spent together.

Ragan fondly remembered the occasion they talked about rough edges. She admitted that her telephone manners were mostly shameful, but only with persistent, rude, or incompetent conversationalists. It was one of a few problems she tried to guard herself against but invariably reverted to her alter ego. It was beneficial to discuss those rough edges in an attempt to refine them, but in the past she would have relived her flaws endlessly. When she announced that she didn't think we'd spend time in heaven replaying rough edges so it made no sense to do so on earth, Kecia saw great hope in a newfound ability to let things go that used to gnaw at her. There was no rule that said she had to carry that load.

It was amazing how many topics they had covered over their lifetime and specifically these last few years of intense dialogue. A lot of things were still unresolved, but Ragan was grateful for any guidance she received and may have shared. She felt fortunate to have this relationship.

On the night before she was to meet with Kecia and let her know what she had decided, Ragan was still apprehensive. She was enjoying a lot of still rather new freedoms. Matters she used to consider important were no longer when she truly searched her heart. She now had the tenacity and vision to change her definition of life. The goal was to know it so well that nothing could sidetrack her only answer.

In the quiet of the night she was reminded of a verse. "Right now we see only through tinted glass, but someday we will see God face to face. This day my understanding is incomplete, but I will see everything unmistakably in full view, as God sees me at this moment."

This is where she was on all these matters, and if everyone else was on a completely different page, they too would have an opportunity to receive answers, and they are where they are today. Perhaps by sharing her beliefs, someone could help her with these questions, and perhaps she could help them. But she was okay with where she was and would be ecstatic if chosen. She looked forward to meeting again with Kecia and the next day in preparation wrote the verse on a card to give to her as her answer.

Kecia was confident that Ragan had been on a nostalgic tour over the past two weeks and was eager to see her friend. Ragan explained how she had spent this time thinking about all their interactions, replaying all their efforts towards resolution, and still wondering if all the answers they had reached versus the questions still pending were enough to tip the scale. "With all the signs around me and everything I've learned and experienced, and the fact that we are created to be like God, you would think trusting Him would be effortless. This holiness is a --" Ragan hesitated. Kecia knew where she was going but thought it would be better if she could finish her own sentence. "This holiness is a conundrum. I know it's been taken care of for me, presented, affirmed and confirmed, taught and accepted, delivered. I would like to not interfere with all that provision."

She handed her card to Kecia and stated, "Someday everything will make sense. Until then, I accept the answers God has given to me."

Kecia understood her heart when she read the card and was thrilled with her answer. "I'm certain God is delighted with your zealous pursuit of His truth. Trust that as murky as it seems, it does make sense, and that is enough. The answers will be there with perfect timing.

"And who wouldn't want some help with all these questions and put to rest those that are unanswerable?"

Journal

Miron

Aaron attended the community music concert and was disappointed but not surprised that he didn't see Miron, his longtime teaching friend. It was the biggest event of the year, and Miron usually played a central role. Every year for the last several Aaron watched as his former colleague's involvement lessened in many of the music events that he was known for organizing. Miron's full-time position was director of music for the high school, and the two usually spoke at the functions Aaron attended in order to stay in touch with the people where he used to work. On recent occasions Miron appeared as though he wasn't enjoying as much both the performances and his part in them. He had been dealing with medical issues for quite some time now, and Aaron could see how much it was affecting him.

Miron was devoted to his teaching and continually encouraged others to take greater roles simply for the love of the arts. He thrived on young minds learning through repetition and aspiring to their highest capabilities, and he saw them all as a masterpiece. He had done some writing of music and had studied it with varying levels of interest throughout his life but primarily was involved with pieces from other writers. His constant exposure to music was for him a tool to learn about people.

His passion for the industry was easily matched by his desire to perform as a concert pianist. He cared for his audience and was often overcome with emotion while playing for them. Once in a while he would forget the piece he was playing as a result of being completely focused on each note. Sometimes he used that intense concentration as a coping mechanism to keep his emotions in check as he was consumed with the music he was trying to release. Many times he was so engrossed in connecting with his beloved listeners, he would finish a song and not remember playing it. He called it an instrumental coma.

It was almost as fulfilling to give his music away as it was to perform it. This he labeled musical Robin Hood. He invoiced appropriately those who could pay for his services and provided them at no cost whenever possible. It was hard to believe he was actually compensated for simply playing. Undoubtedly, his richest performances were for individuals who were blind, from whom he learned to truly see. He recognized everyone as having their own disability. He certainly did, and he was anxious for a time when all music could be heard by everyone and he could be free of his personal weaknesses.

Miron knew every life was composed with complete inspiration and brilliance, including his. There are no missing notes or extra keys. All the imposed rules of proper format don't apply. A dozen verses and no chorus, lyrics that don't rhyme, too loud, too soft, how easy it is for even the untrained professional to hear the flaws. When there is a bad note or a long pause or an ill-placed stanza, when a life seems wholly out of tune, it doesn't matter. It's music, inspired, and there's beauty in it all. Maybe the ears need the adjustment.

Aaron didn't always listen to Miron's music from the audience. He used to hold some of his substitute teaching classes in the room adjacent to Miron's studio. They coordinated efforts to keep to a minimum any potential distraction from learning, but there were not many times when Aaron's students didn't prefer the comforting background music.

Aaron delighted in listening to the student interaction and hearing the progressing talent. In between classes and when no apprentice needed his guidance, Miron could be heard practicing his own improvisation. Many times Aaron sat in the back of the auditorium after school and listened to various rehearsals, and he often was asked to pay a visit backstage to support both novice and professional.

For some time before Aaron left for his new position, he had noticed Miron was frequently absent and refrained from his usual lengthy time of personal enjoyment while playing the piano. They talked about his struggles with his health and prayed together on many occasions.

Miron could never do enough for people, by his own definition, which led to him doing too much. He was mindful of his age playing a role in his decline, but the greater frustration stemmed from his inability to tune out the pain. It was obvious that he was not able to do as much, and he was unable to do anything without discomfort, so he set out to change some well-established but destructive routines. He didn't realize the damage he had been doing all these years.

Every ergonomic possibility he could imagine was explored, in addition to what was suggested to him by friends and physicians, as well as anything available in the industry. Some of his new patterns were remarkably automatic. He was amazed that although the transition was not graceful or pleasant, he could learn again. When tempted to return to what was previously programmed, he thought about both the delight in the changes he had made that were already now effortless and the potential long-term benefit of those changes. At times the modification occurred happily because the original routine was no longer an option and seemed illogical now anyway.

Miron was in it for the long haul. He was now sensitive to recognizing others who were hurting and found a peace in offering a prayer on their behalf. When he observed musicians, he extended a prayer of preservation and praise for the talent bestowed. This was carried forward to anyone he noticed whose task required physical stamina. He was grateful for the miracles he had personally received, and even if no one knew what he went through to get those notes to ring out in order to bless his audience as a whole and each individual within, God knew.

Each part of his music that he slowly relinquished represented more of himself. Some he yielded in disappointment, some in anger, and some with the hope that if he chose to surrender it, it might hurt less. He began giving away pieces that he knew he would probably never be able to play again, knowing that a lot of people have to give something up before they are ready, and understanding that he was fortunate to have experienced this for the time that he did.

It was obvious to him that he had to push through this. If it was easily resolved, where is the faith in that? He felt complete trust is natural to exhibit when your life seems to be in order. Despite his knowledge that there's an unchanging and loving Father who's got this covered, this pain had taken him to places in his faith he didn't think possible, highs and lows. With a little minor healing, the hope soared, and with a little minor regression, the confidence plummeted.

With each visit to the doctor, he was less into the good God could do with this and more into his own anguish. He knew from day one it was better to be at the altar than in the waiting room and didn't neglect either, but with all the tests and treatments, prescriptions and procedures, equipment and aids, specialists and therapists, he still had no diagnosis. The effort to heal one part of his body caused injury to another.

106

The medical visits were time-consuming, as was the constant mental and verbal deliberation in an attempt to find resolution. With a significant investment in time, money, and effort, his return was a substantial stack of medical documents, a cabinet full of half-used bottles, and a box full of little-used apparatus.

He was caught between one insurance company who didn't want to pay if he wasn't able to work for a time and another who didn't want to pay for services in an effort to restore his health. The industry has done a lot of good in the world, but the whole premise is taking care of people, not profits. His theory was that years ago when there was no insurance, people helped each other in a time of crisis. A small town became big enough that they needed an administrator. Someone filed a claim they shouldn't have, and someone denied someone they shouldn't have, and now it's become a monstrosity all about the profit. If there's that much excess, they should pay claims or reduce rates. They should be an administrator, not a bloated middle man.

All the medication left him in a perpetual state of exhaustion. His family had to coordinate a lot of team effort through this, and he was concerned their memories of him would be dominated by this stage. Through his pain and confusion and growing bitterness, he spewed angry words towards his spouse, and there was grace returned, and when there was not, it was just one broken individual hurting for another. The losses continually deepened, lost time and memories, lost function, and ultimately loss of hope. Everything became hollow.

Aaron was aware of how much Miron looked forward to the annual concert, so when he didn't even make an appearance, he tried contacting him and left a message, but Miron did not return his call. Aaron walked by a medical clinic that week just as Miron was exiting, and the two met outside. When Miron saw him approaching, he immediately felt guilty for not returning his phone call and before even saying hello apologized and explained that he just wasn't at a place where he could be the best company with anyone. Aaron assured him that he understood and told him he simply prayed for him rather than with him.

Miron's usual look of appreciation was not there. "So many people have prayed, and I'm blessed to be on every one of those lists, but I don't know what to pray anymore. I know you've gone to bat for me. Words can't express the awesome advocate you are. I do believe that every prayer is answered, sometimes right away and sometimes not for years. The answer could be different than the request, and sometimes the answer is no.

"This is not mind over matter and the power of positive thinking. There have been incredible faith-filled people who have not recovered from a life-threatening disease. I'm fighting a combination of things that are hard to diagnose and treat. I have to be okay with the timing.

"When I study a verse that says, 'There shall no harm come to you,' I'm confused. My weakness, His strength; keep asking, keep seeking, keep knocking, it all seems futile. None of this makes sense anymore. I just don't have anything left, and I want to live without this cloud that has taken up residence over my soul."

Aaron was honored that his friend could still be boldly honest with him even though they had not spent as much time together recently. He asked Miron if he had time to meet with him over at the auditorium where they used to spend hours conversing. He briefly observed Miron's usual look of appreciation and said to him, "I know how hard you've tried to follow God's intention. Let me help you get through this."

If ever there was a place where Miron could connect and feel comfortable, it was here in this auditorium. He still cherished being here despite its current painful reminders. As he spoke, his voice became weak and his words delayed. It was obvious to Aaron how crushing this was to him.

Frequently throughout their conversation Miron stretched in awkward and conspicuous motions, and it appeared as though he had been doing this for so long that he didn't realize how noticeable it was. He was fidgety and often clutched different parts of his body that obviously were painful. At various times he held his glass of ice water against those same areas, and the distress was transparent through his countenance. It had been quite some time since they had really talked, and Aaron perceived he needed to unload an awful lot of misery he had been carrying.

Miron spoke first. "Years ago this pain seemed strangely holy and intimate. My fears of where this could lead were calmed by being in this state of desperate need continually and sensing God was standing by my bedside and sometimes would just curl up beside me to get me through this. I do not fear death after feeling this presence in the midst of physical torment.

"When I needed assurance, sometimes daily, I would receive an affirmation in some form or another, a note of encouragement, a message of prayer, a song with special meaning, an element of nature serving as a clear reminder of Who to trust, an open or closed door, a small step forward.

"I have tried to approach my music as ministry and worship. My job is to provide sound, but my ministry is to love my audience. I have been thankful that God allowed me to live this life and have watched others need to rely on His strength as they fulfilled their calling as well. I understand how difficult equality is, and I also appreciate that God has designed us to need and help each other. This is now the way it is. It is not potentially terminal, and even if it were, may I handle it with a fraction of the grace of those I have watched bravely live despite being stripped of abilities. The aging process alone is a stripping away of life.

"This piano and auditorium have become a big part of who I am. I miss being in the game. My personality doesn't like warming the bench. I'm thankful this has been a slow process, but I'm still not ready to part with everything that is already gone. There's grace and there's time, and the changes are sometimes too subtle for my impatience, but they are worthwhile changes.

"I made a commitment with my gift, and I also made a commitment to part with it if asked to do something else. The direction is not illusive. It's just not something I can comprehend. I know God has called me to continue as long as he tells me to continue. I will keep asking, and I will accept the answer.

"I have studied the servant Job and the many faces I witness around me who appear to be in as much torture as he was, and my plight seems miniscule compared to the suffering of others, but I look at the cross, and sometimes the will of God seems cruel. The moment that was most wrenching was when Jesus felt abandoned.

"Again and again I have recalled a message that has stayed with me. It was about the three men who were thrown into the blazing furnace for refusing to bow to something false. Their response continually was, 'I know my God is able, and I know He will, and even if He doesn't, I'm not bowing.'

"I laid claim to that message and repeated it silently and aloud until it rolled off my tongue like 'please' and 'thank you.' And then I bowed, and then I broke. And God lifted and repaired. Then I broke enough times that I quit asking to be repaired. I resented who and what I used to love because of the pain and its duration and the constant need to recycle the hope that had been trashed only yesterday. I didn't want to be a part of this plan. I reminded God that those three trusting and faithful men didn't spend seven years in that furnace and certainly didn't have equivalent pain. Not one hair on them was even singed.

"Part of me is ashamed that this has beaten me down to this level, and part of me feels like who wouldn't be here after all this. I'm disappointed that I broke at all. I lost the opportunity to show where my trust lies and respond accordingly. I am also disappointed that with all the changes, I still contributed to this by taking on too much, out of fear.

"I have laid in bed, reciting over and over a passage in Psalm 23, as though I am still trying to remind God of his Word, and I question whether it applies to me. 'Surely goodness and mercy shall follow me all the days of my life, and I will dwell in the house of the Lord forever.'"

The delay before Miron's next words was considerable. He closed his eyes and shed several tears. When he looked up, he radiated this expression as if he had just solved his own equation. Aaron was still listening intently and had not spoken one word but was inspired by the transformation he observed.

Miron confidently continued, "I perceive that 'Surely goodness' is defined in a realm above my comprehension. It's what happens when God redeems these losses and exchanges them for eternal value. I have spent the last seven years trying to find healing. My humanness wrestles with this. My soul is all right with every single minute of it. It's what I know, not what I feel."

His voice was stronger, but his words formed slowly, like he was attempting to ascend a cliff with each utterance, hand

111

over hand, word over word. Aaron had not missed one syllable or one tear.

"I'm desperate to find purpose. Perhaps I'll teach more, study and write more music. My gift is in my head, not my body. Many people lose parts of their lives. The parts that remain are a gift. It would be regretful not to use them. Why wouldn't I use this gift to do something eternal? Without the loss, there would be no pursuit of a new dream. This will not enslave me or consume me. I've been embraced by my Father."

Just a few moments earlier Aaron's request would have been inappropriate, but now it would be inconceivable to not offer to him this enormous opportunity. "Miron, I don't want you to answer me today, but I'd like to tell you about a project we are working on at the Jenski Museum. The owner announced that there's just time and space for one more biography, so we are interviewing several candidates, and then there will be a selection process. I'd like you to think about sharing your story."

Miron this time without delay replied, "I've talked so much and to so many about this, family, friends, and I think pretty close to every doctor in the city, but if it would bring meaning to this suffering and lost season, I'll share my story. Maybe the medical visits would serve to enhance other physicians' understanding of any future patients facing some of the same challenges. I am hopeful this will encourage someone and they are able to avoid some of this anguish. To go through this for the value of another soul, it's worth it. It's what was done for me.

"But you know, this isn't the great comeback story that we all appreciate reading. Those are stories of pushing through adversity, ending in ultimate triumph."

Aaron acknowledged and put to rest Miron's concern. "No, it isn't the perfect comeback story just waiting to be published in hard cover and stored on film as well, but it's probably closer to reality for most of us. As dramatic and beloved as those stories are, in the back of your mind you kind of know the ending is the ultimate triumph or they wouldn't have recorded the story. There are plenty of those out there. We need to hear also about the one who finished second or couldn't finish at all but gave it everything. Those stories reshape lives too.

"Yours is not the overnight miracle, but it resembles tests and trials. You have determined to continue and push through adversity without regard to an ultimate triumph, to be vigilant and seek advice and receive continual healing.

"You're more familiar with giving assignments than receiving them, but I'd love to meet with you here again sometime next week after you've had occasion to reflect on everything we've discussed and possibly organize your thoughts."

When Aaron arrived the next week for their meeting, there was music in the auditorium, a recording of Miron's that included some of his community and student events. They sat and listened and reminisced, and then Miron handed to Aaron his assignment. Since they both were teachers, it was not the least bit odd that he documented his life discoveries in outline format.

His voice was again weak and his words delayed, but this time for different reasons. "I found a tremendous correlation between the body and the soul when dealing with illness and healing. I think anybody in the medical field is fortunate to be in a position to behold this every day, but I believe every industry can be an instrument for God to be revealed. Everyone with repetitive injury, whether physical, emotional, professional, or social, has the same opportunity for their soul to receive redemptive healing through their suffering."

113

Aaron read and studied the outline while they listened to Miron's performances.

Repetitive Injury, Redemptive Healing

Our heart plays a central role in the healing of our soul, and every vessel, including the tiniest connection at the furthest extremity, without nourishment from its source will die.

In order to receive true healing for the body and soul, both the cause and symptoms need to be treated. A diagnosis explains the damage and pain, and it guides the treatment.

The medical records file can become too heavy to carry, just as the years of damage to our soul are too much to handle on our own. We want to keep going and we want to quit.

Proper care of both body and soul sometimes occurs only out of necessity, and injury can often be a blessing leading to desirable changes.

Weaknesses and strengths can be congenital or hereditary. We may not even be aware that there's a problem.

Deep healing from repetitive and chronic injury requires a great amount of work, patience, and sacrifice. A little faith doesn't hurt either.

Nutrition and a balance between rest and activity are essential. We shouldn't starve or stuff the body or soul. Fatigue leaves us vulnerable to injury. A good workout provides health and strength. Inactivity leads to clots and sores.

Now and then we stop short of the goal. Sometimes we want no goal at all in order to avoid disappointment and failure.

It is best to prevent injury. It is wise to deal with it immediately to prevent it from getting worse. Maintenance is necessary to prevent reoccurrence.

Health affects our emotions and appearance. It requires losing bad habits and gaining good ones. Retraining feels unnatural, but pain is an indicator that it is urgent.

If broken, it doesn't matter how or how much or for how long; we are designed to heal. There may be scarring or loss of function, but permanence does not last beyond this lifetime.

As the body ages, the soul is designed to mature.

We can be over-preventative, snap under pressure, or self-destructive. We are tested, retested, and at times pushed to the limits.

When we are in pain, we are vulnerable to false promises, and we'll do anything for relief. We search out medication for the body and soul. Drugs can be healing, alleviating, masking, or addicting.

Pain is consuming and debilitating. We can pretend it doesn't hurt only so long. Chronic pain of our soul affects our body, and chronic pain of our body affects our soul.

Illness keeps us from growing. The immunity that comes from within is better than a shot. Relief from pain increases appreciation for life.

No one is immune from pain. One out of every six people has chronic physical pain. The number of people with pain in their soul is immeasurable.

We all want a quick fix and a grand story. At times that gift is granted, and other times it is measured out daily. Sometimes the gift lies in what we find in our desperate search.

Regression in healing of the body and soul is not unlike experiencing springtime followed by a snowstorm.

We stop at nothing to heal and save a life. We are made in the image of God.

Everyone in both industries is called to help people. There's only one Primary Care Provider.

After having read his outline, Aaron received Miron's permission to forward a copy of it to the museum and then adamantly concluded, "This isn't about bringing some sort of purpose to everything that has happened to you. That's not your job. Look at the change in your soul, even when it may have felt like it was faltering. That is the miracle that you have been seeking, and that is the finer reason to enter your story. Who wouldn't want that kind of healing?"

Journal

The Last Biography

A text came through to both Kecia and Aaron directly from the owner. Generally if he needed to communicate with them, he called them in order to keep their relationships on a more intimate level. This choice of expedited contact had to mean something. This phase of their efforts was complete. The text message unpretentiously stated, "It is time." They did not need to hear his voice to identify with the exhilarating atmosphere that must be present at the museum as Garrick looked forward to editing his last piece and Jaimin anticipated finally completing his collection that would be without a doubt award-winning.

Kecia and Aaron were inundated with emotion at the thought of introducing all their stories but wasted no time making arrangements and contacting each of them to broadcast details of the announcement. Aaron had kept quite an extensive journal of his time spent gathering information regarding the three applicants he submitted for this last biography. It would be awesome to look back and discover why he believed so strongly in these candidates. Kecia had chosen not to use her journal at all. Both in their own way were reviewing their points of view and mentally preparing for additional input to provide to the owner since they would be asked for their recommendation and their choice.

They had been wondrously favored to have found each of the lives they personally encountered, and they had diligently monitored the weekly correspondence updating the entire team on its progress, so they were aware of the number of entrants of high caliber. It would almost have to be more about what was missing in the collection than who these people were because the possible choices were too great. Perhaps it would be decided best based on whose story would help the most people. They were glad they didn't have to ultimately choose and trusted the owner to make the right decision.

The day had finally arrived when it would be revealed who was chosen. Arrangements were made to bring each participant to the airport. Kecia and Aaron thought it entirely appropriate to charter a plane and then provide a limousine for the final leg of the trip to the Jenski Museum.

Adlai's parents accompanied her for the ride to the airport and then were honored to let her go on her own the rest of the way. It was a great privilege for Matthew's parents to represent their son in this journey. Peter's wife had been an integral part of this process as well, so she was invited to attend the day's festivities. The couple boarded a connecting flight that departed on time and arrived in time to meet up with the rest of the group. It had just been a few weeks since Kecia had completed her work with Peter, but they all three reunited as if it had been once again decades. Kecia proudly introduced the couple to everyone present.

While the aircraft was en route, they all had time to briefly connect with each other's story. No one was assessing their own value compared with another, and there was no anxiety over who would be chosen. They instantly bonded because of their shared experience, opportunity, and good fortune to have just been an important part of this phenomenal adventure, knowing the impact would reach far beyond any contest.

Halfway through the ride, Rhesa noticed that Kecia was savoring every detail of the moment surrounding her. She was scanning the airplane to appreciate what was taking place, and

Rhesa asked her what was on her mind. Kecia told her she was thinking about how much Garrick adores this stuff, the fact that all of these individuals came from separate circumstances and are now here together learning about each other and how their paths have crossed.

While in the limousine Colson of course had his camera at the ready for the moment he got his first glimpse of the Jenski Museum. He could tell they were getting close by the look on Kecia's and Aaron's faces. He thought highly of Aaron after getting to know him so well through their apprenticeship of sorts, yet he was unexpectedly attached to Kecia as well. Her smile and the life in her eyes overwhelmed him. Simply being near her generated a festive mood.

Aaron had talked about his colleagues many times. It was unclear who was more excited, the team members who had been waiting in the wings, the candidates, or the staff who would get to introduce them.

Colson knew how fortunate he was to be chosen for this experience. He had a tough time choosing which picture to take. He knew the museum could be photographed at any point, but he was torn between catching the group's reaction or Kecia's and Aaron's celebration as they escorted their treasured stories to the entrance. Colson was completely lost in their expression of love, was stable in his gaze but trembled too much to photograph anything when he saw the Jenski he had heard so much about, its brilliant owner, and his trusted editor standing next to him, both anxiously waiting to welcome everyone.

Introductions were almost not necessary, and a handshake was far too formal. Every attempt to force time into slow motion and linger in the moment was defeated by an uncontrollable desire to explore the endless museum contents and learn more about each of its team members.

Jaimin asked his editor and staff to lead everyone to the room with the space for just one more biography. They gathered inside and were eager to read the various titles. Each person appreciated the enormity of the collection and couldn't help but stare at the one remaining spot void of a story, and they all took a moment to reflect on their desire to be a part of the collection and why. They were reminded of the assignment.

"Only one space left, one empty place on the shelf to fill. The collection had been decades in the making, and now it was almost finished. Just one more. All the planning and preparation, energy and sacrifice were culminating in perfection. There was only time and space for one more book. This would be a special book, the last biography.

"The project was close to completion. The museum was near capacity, and soon there would be the long-awaited ceremony to dedicate a life's work and commitment. Without doubt, the owner had planned something unpredictable.

"More than one generation had been guests of the Jenski Museum and had watched others as they were changed by the experience as well. They learned about the past and reflected on their own lives as they read the biographies of others. Each piece archived held special meaning for many. Hours of joy filled these halls. The museum was an extension into the community, a gift.

"Its owner was highly regarded because of the contents of this acclaimed historical structure, and the famed museum was highly regarded because of its impassioned owner, Jaimin. He collected art and artifacts as well, but only those pieces which reminded him of his books, especially those where he took part in the writing. Those cherished books were the focus of his attention. It consumed all his time. He started with only one, and over the years it became an incredible collection.

122

"He wanted there to be a connection between the readers and the stories. They were to be inclusive and diverse and cover every life experience, occupation, and personality type he could conceive. There were books dedicated to the powerful and powerless. There were accounts of kings and scholars and every talent imaginable. It was important to include such variety that anyone who walked through the doors could find something that spoke to their heart. His collection was still missing something.

"The owner had asked his editor to complete just one more biography. Garrick's heart pounded as he walked by the place where the last book was to go. He experienced this every time he began a new project, but this was different. The dream of his finished work would propel him through the process.

"Jaimin opened the doors to the conference room with great resolution. His team was present, and as anticipated, he announced, 'This is it! This will be the last biography. After all of these years working together, we're so close to accomplishing this dream. We'll interview for and edit and place on the shelf just one more biography before the dedication we've been longing to experience together.'

"Jaimin especially adored the unexpected."

There would be no long and arduous process of elimination, just a joyous announcement of the selection. Staff was confident that they knew who would be chosen. The owner had perhaps confided in them previous to this gathering. Garrick as well appeared to be aware of the choice. Jaimin invited him to make the announcement since he had worked so hard to make it all possible.

Garrick spoke with all the authority granted to him. "The last biography is

You!"

Jaimin added the improbable element that this indicates not just the seven fictional characters but the reader of this book as well.

All of the hopefuls were too euphoric to wonder how this could be possible. For right now, they were just ecstatic that Jaimin, whose name means "I love," was inclusive and had found a way for them to be a part of this extraordinary legacy.

They celebrated and congratulated, and then Garrick, whose name means "power," continued, "Your lives are treasured because you have always belonged here with us. Your membership has been donated and your trust in the organization acknowledged. Kecia and Aaron have given you a glimpse into something that you long for, heaven."

The newest Jenski members were all still a little breathless and certainly bewildered at the outcome of their experience. Aaron and Kecia had been looking forward to revealing the significance of everything that was taking place, who they all truly are and who this book is really about.

Aaron, whose name means "enlightened," stepped into his role as educator and ably pronounced, "The Editor is the Owner's Son, and you are the Owner's children as well. He sent us to be with you. The Owner is your Author, but you may also address him as Dad. This is a family business.

"In keeping with our assignment, there is time for one more, and there is one more empty place on the shelf to fill. Just one more, and then just one more. Yours is a special book, the last biography. These cherished books are the focus of His attention. It consumes all His time. His collection is still missing something. The Owner asks his Editor to complete just one more biography. 'We'll interview for and edit and place on the shelf just one more biography before the dedication we've been longing to experience together.'"

Kecia, whose name means "great joy," stepped into her role as sustainer and happily announced, "Aaron and I wanted to tell each of you but had to wait until we could tell all of you. We recognize some of the same qualities in you that we love about Jaimin and Garrick. The Owner fell in love with your story when we submitted the list of candidates. He doesn't have anything even close to your storyline in His collection. He asked the Editor about you personally and requested that we make contact with you."

Jaimin expressed further his intimate relationship. "It will be infinitely visible to you through this experience that you are my very own. Your lives have been perfectly edited by my Son and completely refined by my Spirit. Aaron and Kecia have been your teacher and comforter, but they are not just for a chosen few, nor are they given to the spiritually elite, whether self-defined or by the world's standards. The Spirit is for all mankind."

The number of Staff symbolizes two prominent roles of the Holy Spirit, comforter and teacher. Since people are created in the image of God, Aaron and Kecia represent the male and female qualities of the Creator. The time spent with Staff is any encounter with the Spirit or someone or something that exemplifies the Spirit, any time of connection set aside to pursue this relationship or just to be still and listen.

The first, last, and only biography that needed no editing was Jesus, and then He edited every other biography who asked. The time Garrick spent interviewing depicts His three years of ministry on earth before being promoted to Editor, which He is now wholly qualified for because of the cross. His workshop was for His years as a carpenter. As Archivist, He is not willing to overlook or lose even one of His prized pieces.

Jaimin portrayed a proprietor with everything, except the missing piece of His collection, aching for just one more. He is the Owner and Author and is the only writer who allows the story to decide its next sentence and the end of the book. He is more a Coauthor, graciously authorizing us to partner with Him in the manuscript.

The Team is the Trinity. Without the Owner and Author, there's no story. Without the Editor and Archivist, there's no collection, and the books contain a lot of unprocessed stuff that doesn't make for a good read, a fine production, or anything close to the happily ever after that is our source of hope. The Archivist puts everything in its place. Without the Staff, there's no liaison and no way to see the truth.

The Jenski Museum, whose name means "coming home," is any place where the Trinity is present. As incredible a place as the museum is, it is just a satellite office, to take care of some things before we arrive at the home office, something to grasp now to have a vision of then. Fatigue will never set in, and there are no time or budgetary constraints. The dedication is the transformation in heaven when the mission is complete.

The invaluable collection is the kingdom. The priceless books are His people. Without souls, the building is empty. Each book will be read and celebrated by many, but it was authored and edited and nurtured by the Trinity. There is nothing more significant than this legacy.

Fiction turns to reality. "The Last Biography is You." Put the seven hopefuls in this book on pause for as long as you need. Insert your name and the details grand and trivial of your own life. There's nothing better than a true story. The Author desires that each reader knows unconditionally He speaks of you. How bold of Him to ask that every last one of His possessions has a book on a shelf in this life written for and about them. The request has not been denied.

Better still, Psalm 139:16, "Your eyes saw every part of me before I was even born. Each moment of my life was inscribed in Your book." Each of His possessions has a book on an eternal shelf, autographed only by faith, authored and owned by the Father, edited and preserved by His Son, influenced and pursued by the Spirit.

"The Last Biography" is not extravagant, but the eternal book will be beautifully bound and illustrated. Not one copy will be sold, but it will be on the best-read list. Any awards won will give praise to the Trinity. If film is preferred over print, that can be arranged. When edited and put to music, no life is beneath a prize-winning production. Every story is significant and has a designated place on a prominent shelf in a well-kept library, museum, or registered historic place.

Whether you kept track mentally or on the pages provided, was there one of the seven fictional characters you wanted to be chosen? There were various ages and attributes and problems, the economy, war, education, health, growing up, relationships.

Were you drawn to someone like you or an individual similar to somebody in your life? Maybe they were inspirational or even opposite your personality and experiences, good and bad. Perhaps they touched a nerve.

Possibly you felt the one who had accomplished the most by human standards was the only deserving one. These people were just too ordinary and not nearly special enough to have a respected Archivist make room for them in a revered historic collection. The Owner treasured "books dedicated to the powerful and powerless." It is unimaginable that God would hold such a place of distinction and purpose for us in His kingdom and in His heart.

It could be that you thought it was unfair to have to choose at all and you believed everyone was deserving of the honor. You just knew they all would have to somehow be included because their lives were unique and the museum would be missing something remarkable without them.

What evidence did you want to be the most important when it came to deciding? If you picked a favorite character, did they resemble you or a person you desire to emulate? The Team picked you.

This book is entirely symbolic. Read into every detail and tilt it upwards. Run it all by the Spirit. Consider doing as Aaron told Colson. "Write all over the pages. Take a red correcting pen to everything you believe doesn't fit or doesn't fit you. Question it. Search out your truth. Find a way to uncover what does fit you. It is only true freedom of speech if it is free of judgment. Share it with somebody you trust or reflect on it inwardly. The gift of being in someone's presence or just knowing how they would respond fuels personal development. You can choose to be who you are embellished by all the good qualities you have learned from those around you."

The seven aspirants had always possessed incredible qualities, but in the presence of the Staff and Team everyone has the ability to exhibit traits that are a testament to God creating us in His likeness and inhabiting us through His Spirit. Despite our imperfections, we are invited not only to be part of the collection but members of the Team as well. Changes transpire in every willing life, and Godly traits can't help but bloom persistently and brilliantly.

If the candidates seemed a little unrealistic, without the expected muck that is generally deemed as necessary to be highly entertaining, conceivably it is because that has already been edited and put in its proper place. It was all there, all the rough drafts and every canvas we want to paint over and every piece of footage we want to erase. It was just seen through the eyes and the filter of the Editor.

They had issues to edit and priorities in disarray, but it was the candidates, not the Team, with the need to get the stuff out of the way and/or bring something good to the table before entering the room. None of it matters and all of it matters. Strip it away and there's still a life, someone to fill what would otherwise be an empty and heavy-hearted chasm.

With grace and redemption, everyone has a rags to riches story, tragedy to triumph. Every life holds adventure and intrigue, but we only know about the lives of those in the past who have recorded or who have been recorded, which leaves the rest of humanity sometimes questioning their earthly significance. There is purpose to reading all about the designed in this life. It is to learn about the Designer. It is better to be validated by the Universe than the world. "Each moment of my life was inscribed in Your book." Every story of grace is chronicled.

Perhaps scholarly faith is esteemed because under it all we're just hoping to be adequate. Most of the characters from the book struggled with being good enough to publish. At times it is easier to think of ourselves as a fictional character, stand back and see the truth in someone else. Who would want to read anything I have to say, or even more puzzling, who would want to read anything about my life? What higher audience than the

Team? They wrestled with importance, adequacy, and purpose. Anything that would have been too heavy or would have held them back had already been dealt with by the Editor. A young child can take this journey. There's no need to toil to attain merit. What the Designer has created is not just good enough, it's good.

This is not about timelines of faith and receiving the gift. It's coming to a place of complete devotion. Here's my story, here's my life. Edit and own it. Let it be a display of Your design. Let it resonate this place in Your heart. God would find a way to get the world what it needed. He was just giving them the opportunity to participate, and the benefit for them was immeasurable.

Most of them had obstacles in the way. Peter needed closure for a painful part of his life before he was able to move forward. Adlai represented a childlike faith when it was easy to give of ourselves. Schedules didn't interfere, and other ventures were not more interesting or validating. Matthew committed and gave his life, but it was his love for God that meant far more than the giving of his life. Colson did not feel complete. He wasn't there yet. Rhesa thought her love story was too broken. Her love was not noble enough to give. Ragan had too many unanswered questions. Miron was in pain and felt abandoned, and he was desperate to redeem his own losses, which was a mistaken motivation.

Maybe there were times when Staff seemed inconsistent. They were highly philosophical and theological in some of their relationships and not in others. They were not wavering or spiritually timid. They understood what each person needed in order to see the truth, and they were persistent.

The candidates were privileged to go on field trips and photo shoots with the Spirit, experience memories and self-discovery and dinner with a friend. They fell in love with the Staff, and in turn with the Team. Whether through nature or photography or music, alone or in the presence of Staff, the Spirit spoke to them and helped them believe in the Editor and experience oneness with the Team.

Much has been written and produced concerning the Owner, Editor, and the angels. The Spirit is mysterious, frequently misunderstood, but not illusive. It's more everyone and everywhere and everyday than breath. If we often become like those around us, how awesome to tap into this infinite strength.

No one is more interested in every chapter, page, and word of our life than the only nonfictional superhero. He rose to the challenge of putting our life in perfect order under any circumstance. If used for good, every movie with a superhero is a visual representation of the provision for every soul. The real superhero never doubts His calling, never fails the mission, and includes all of mankind in the rescue.

Inasmuch as we are fashioned after the Owner, we can perceive His desire to give and receive love and companionship and affirmation. He created the novel and the screen and the canvas and the stage, and He welcomes us to His own debut daily. With everything He has, what is missing is still unsettling. His idea of unity was the garden and is heaven, and He aches for us when reality is far from either, and yet He is waiting, allowing freewill to bring us together, and holding out for a missing life.

The Team is the finest example of a genuine collaboration. If its members sounded too good to be true, this is based on a true story, based on a true Book. There are just a few Biblical references included at the end of this book. It's not such a fictional impossibility. The intention was not to trivialize the Deity but to try to understand it in this world searching for answers, through contemporary personalities that we can get to know and love. If the influence is positive, then the collection and the Team are blessed.

Without our love, the once regal story is an Owner with an empty museum, an Editor without a story to redeem, a Comforter without a soul to console, a Teacher without an apprentice eager to learn and grow and perpetuate the story.

We've perhaps been to the museum before. Its purpose may not have been as clear then. It's just a glimpse. In a deep part of God's heart is the excitement of planning and preparing a gift for His children. We can imagine building a home or planning a special occasion for and with someone, dreaming of their delight in what we have done for them and then realizing their hope to share it with someone else and echo their own memories.

Even the most incredible life here on earth is nothing compared to eternity. There's no need to spend time vying to be mortally significant when eternal importance is available. This is the only reality that matters. Everyone is invited to partake. No one has to settle for a consolation prize. No one goes home. Well, everyone goes home! No one is excluded or has their dreams dashed. There's no need for added drama to make the story. The truth is dramatic enough. Gentle, constructive criticism and high praise are given by the only completely unneutral yet qualified advocates.

The cameras are focused on the heart, and it wouldn't matter if there was a broadcast for the whole world to watch. In the presence of the Team, the world has no effect on behavior. Nothing is more real than interacting with the Team. Trust in the Editor is the only necessity. The stakes are eternal, the cost is covered, and the prize is unimaginable.

If we turn reality back to fiction, we still have the dilemma of seven stories and one remaining space. The Owner planned for that. He told them all that they had been compelled by His Spirit to be there because they already belonged. The Team is not restricted by mortally imposed boundaries. Space is not limited or constrained by a ceiling, walls, or square footage. The Owner is masterful at creating, and He put on record "Each moment of my life was inscribed in His book." At the Jenski Museum every soul is given more than just one space for a book summarizing their entire life. A room full of books is devoted to each moment of their life.

The Team is also not restrained by time. The chosen dispersed to experience individually their own room, and the entire Team went with them all simultaneously. The guests couldn't wait to behold what words the Author and Editor used to detail their lives. They felt safe, and their hearts were intent on their lives being a beautiful room to the Team and to the world. The rest of the afternoon was spent appreciating life to this point, comforting and teaching, editing and archiving, and writing into the future. The Team was fully present at the same time in every room all afternoon. The Trinity can do that.

Because a lifetime is expanded to a room, an empty place on a shelf can be contracted to an opportunity. There's time and space for one more, just one more. The collection is still missing something. There's still one last opportunity to do something special with the time remaining before the dedication. The possibilities are awesome. Whether adding a word or an entire room, every occasion increases the collection, every word prayed or every soul rescued.

The Rooms

Peter didn't know for certain but suspected he was the closest to returning at the end of his life to his completed room. He no longer needed to relive the bookcase that had caused him to be stagnant. He understood the difference between an intention and an error, and the Spirit had shown him both were well taken care of by the Author and Editor.

In agreement with this freedom, the Team for a few minutes took Peter to a brother's room. The man had no redeeming qualities that we know of, but once in his life he acknowledged the Editor, and the thief on the cross entered paradise with Jesus. Unlike Peter, who had been caught up with one blemish, the thief was defined by one moment of perfection, and it was recorded and has given hope to countless people, and their friends and family, who may have whispered their first prayer with their last breath. It has given peace to those with a passion for souls in believing that it's never too late. His room was full.

Adlai wanted to stay forever and play "Well, why not?" with the whole Team. She was delighted to see how many books already filled her room. It was amazing to read into her life, and the Owner explained that He had the same feeling when anyone read His Book. He reminded her of her love for the horizon rainbow and told her that that was so she would remember that His Son had prepared this place just for her, as promised.

Matthew's parents had many times since he had been gone walked into the room where he grew up and relived as many memories as they could. This room at the Jenski Museum held every last memory of his whole life. They picked up book after book and retold the moments that they had almost forgotten, and they were grateful that the Editor's red markings covered every book contained in this abundant room. Obviously they were hoping that Matthew would come bursting through the doors, but this was enough for now.

Colson was still too enthralled with what was transpiring to be able to photograph it, and he wasn't sure anyway that it would develop, but especially in this case a photo could not begin to do justice. He fell in love with not only the Editor but the privilege of being edited and thought that it closely resembled what a photo undergoes. It wasn't just about erasing flaws and enjoying substance and enhancing qualities. It was the hands-on interaction between the photo and photographer, what they were together, and the strength of the print in His presence.

When the picture started to become blurry to Colson, he was shown where it was that he started to believe something harmful, and he was assured that he was never without a guiding hand. The idea of trying to self-edit or deliberately testing the Editor's capabilities would be defeated by Colson's love for the Team.

Rhesa knew with the picture of happily ever after that she was presented with from this adventure, nothing on earth could even come close, and unless it resembled her experience at the museum or helped her learn more about it, she'd have no part of it. Every disappointment in a temporal relationship was now an incredible opportunity to be embraced by God's perfection. She had been suspicious, but the décor in her room confirmed that the Owner of the Jenski Museum was also the Owner of the cottage where she was restored.

Ragan wanted to stay forever and have all her questions answered, especially with regard to parenting, but she was able to quickly let that notion go when she walked to the stained-glass window and read underneath it an inscription of the verse that encouraged her to take this step.

"Right now we see only through tinted glass, but someday we will see God face to face. This day my understanding is incomplete, but I will see everything unmistakably in full view, as God sees me at this moment."

She was affirmed for not allowing potential public opinion to hinder her from doing what she believed God had asked her to do. She could not endure the thought of placing her fear in front of His will, and if there was one soul to be positively impacted by her story, she would not withhold it.

The room seemed voluminous but appeared no larger from the outside than anyone else's. When she opened up one of the books and commented on the small print, Garrick laughed and told her that since she was a bit wordy, they had to reduce the font through the entire room in order to record her life. He assured her that they had already had that fix in place before she was designed.

Miron, upon entering his room, wept in the arms of the Owner. His tears were accepted wholly as an act of worship. Tears were welcome here, but once everyone approached the home office, there would be no need. As Miron looked through his recent books, it was clear that Aaron had been at every one of his medical appointments, not just coincidentally there once to meet him as he was exiting. It had been hard for him to understand that Aaron was there for him when he didn't experience daily his presence. The Scripture he had time and again recited was effective with Aaron nearby, but in his greatest pain, the Spirit was there, in some form.

He affirmed faith arrives when it doesn't make sense but will someday, even if not on earth. Every temporal experience has eternal value. To trace the meaning of something in the past always makes the Author look brilliant. It will be that way someday with every word, page, and chapter. The losses will be recovered.

Miron's room did not have a great amount of books on the shelves to this point because there was an abundance of music. That collection may have been close to completion. Still, in the center of the room there was an exact replica of his piano.

The Table

The afternoon went by far too quickly, the exploration and reflection and communion with the Team in this holy place. It was just a brief visit, and they knew this feeling but never so intensely. Summer break was over or the family reunion had to wrap up or the dream was interrupted by the alarm clock. It would be very difficult to depart, but unlike any of those feelings, just having been here and knowing now what is waiting would give purpose to a lifetime of preparation. Every hardship on earth could be seen as trivial in light of this reward.

They all sat down at the table that we've dreamed about and heard about, but have realized only a fraction of its beauty in the pictures and songs composed to try to experience it. It didn't matter what was served. The only concern was who was at the table. The gathering was whole when Matthew joined the rest of the group as they broke bread and shared the cup and savored every expression on every face and clung to every word delivered by the Team. The conversation was its own form of music.

The whole Team loved to give, and Jaimin explained to his guests that even though They would always be with them, He understood their need for a physical reminder, something tangible they could hold and go to as a source of strength. The Staff had selected gifts unique to each one of them. This would assist them in their distinct service for the Team. The Owner would accomplish awesome plans in and through their lives. Staff would assure their days would be so rich that everyone around them would benefit as well.

Everyone understood why Kecia started first with Adlai. It was like Christmas, youngest to oldest, and as with Christmas, these gifts would be opened immediately and celebrated by all. It was a small box, and Adlai was too excited to try to guess what it was. Kecia knew she would simply burst if the unwrapping was complicated and tedious, so there was no paper or tape, wires or latches.

Adlai listened to Kecia explain what was inside before it was placed in her hands. "This represents the first miracle ever performed. In the Bible there were many miracles that followed; so too will there be in your life. You will see miracles all around you and be involved in their spectacle." Inside was a miniature globe, a pink miniature globe, a gift that would be opened countless times through her years. This child who saw nothing but possibilities was granted the desire of her heart.

Aaron stood proudly and approached Colson with his gift. It was important that Colson realize that as much as Aaron cherished their work together, their relationship existed well beyond photography, so he purposely avoided presenting anything that symbolized it. He would not allow Colson to be limited by defining himself only through his craft.

Aaron cleared the table and placed a large book in front of him titled "Philosophy." Colson's name was engraved just below the title, and he understood immediately when he opened to the first blank page that it was his journal to author. Aaron instructed his student once again, "Your gift is not limited to a single course of study. Your philosophy will be broad and extensive and will carry you through difficult decisions. You will be sound and solid, rational and reasonable, deep and informed, clearheaded, clearsighted, unbiased, undeceived, well-advised, and well-grounded."

Sweet Rhesa was next. She tried to act as though she wasn't nervous or self-conscious, but this group could pretty much see through anything by now. Kecia hugged her and told her not to shake the box. Surrounded by multicolored and tightly packed tissue was a beautiful aqua-tinted glass vase full of sand. She didn't know yet what it portrayed but excitedly asked, "Is it?" "Yes," Kecia responded. "It is from the place where you spent many days listening to God.

"Your gift is insight. It will guide your heart and change your life. This wisdom will be called upon daily in your new purpose. I happen to know of a job posting meant for you. Your experience makes you more than qualified, and opposite your current position, it is 90% people, 10% administration. The job advertisement no longer lists this as a requirement in its description because it overwhelmed too many applicants. You will be guiding parents and children from an old destructive life to a new abundant one."

Matthew had already been given his gift, when he really needed it. The symbol was given to him by his parents, but it was the Spirit who gave him the gift of faith.

The concept of perhaps needing to identify him with simply a dog tag, as much honor as it held, left JoAnne and Rick hollow, so they purchased a small gold cross on a chain and had his initials engraved on the back. They gave it to him just before he left for training, and they wondered why it was not with the personal effects that were returned to them. They thought maybe he had stored it somewhere so it would be safe, maybe it was taken by someone out of greed, maybe he had given it to someone special.

Matthew opened a leather case with the cross inside and placed it in his mother's hands. "The gift became who I was. I don't need the symbol here. I'm immersed in it." Everyone present, with the exception of the Team and Matthew, had a few tears to wipe away. Garrick remembered what it was like to weep, but since they were now home, He and Matthew both had retired their tear ducts.

JoAnne shed the last tear within the group, and then Aaron spoke directly to Matthew's parents. "This now becomes your symbol, and your gift is speech. You have a story to tell in a manner that will be received. You have been granted a glimpse of heaven and a panoramic view of your son's purpose. You have a story to tell."

Ragan was enjoying so much the unique offerings and the reaction of the recipients, she didn't realize she was the next youngest. She recognized the size and shape of the package Kecia handed to her as a CD holder. She could guess the symbol, but what was the gift? It was still a mystery when she opened it and saw the cover contained a picture of a piano and Miron's name as the artist. Miron was just as curious. Aaron had asked for a copy of some of his work, Miron assumed for his own use, but he was elated to see Kecia use it as her gift. "Ragan, I know how music takes you to a place of calm. Your gift is intuition. You will distinguish between truth and deception. When doubt creeps in, this music is to remind you of the source."

Aaron approached Miron with a small red box and told him the outside and the inside were connected. Inside the box was a single carpenter nail. It wasn't an old rusty nail, but its meaning was obviously more beautiful than its appearance. "Your gift is healing. You've been honored to experience some of the pain of the Editor and understand how even the most remote parts of the body die without a constant flow of blood. Though this season has felt like repetitive injury to your body and soul, there is redemptive healing through the Spirit. Your roots are deeper and your losses will be validated."

Peter, the senior member, was given a postcard with different words, pictures, and symbols on the front. He read it until he recognized one of the words, "amor." He knew very little Spanish but remembered it meant "love." Amy realized that the postcard contained multiple languages with the word "love." Kecia stated, "Love is the symbol. Your gift is language, and Amy will facilitate. You will travel the world and use your gifts to display the love you know in this moment."

Kecia and Aaron entrusted all these attributes to these souls they had followed intently. The Staff explained they all had been selected not just for an adventure or even a season of personal growth but for a lifetime of worship. The tasks they would undertake in their daily lives, whether joyous or heavy, and the relationships they would nurture would bless the Team. They were not dismissed from the Jenski; they were appointed by the Spirit.

They were all so enamored with the gift that had been given to them, they knew they would never look or sound the same again. The preprogrammed rational behavior that seemed natural to them and everyone else just didn't make sense anymore. They hoped there was such a difference that people around them would wonder what had happened, who they were

141

becoming, and what they were talking about. They understood how their lives have abundant purpose and significance. They would be less concerned with the details of life and more concerned with its meaning. Nothing else really mattered.

This encounter changed their direction. Each of them would find themselves in a place of influence with the ability to care for others who also had been captured by the Author's love. Miron spoke for all of the chosen when he stated, "We will always remember how the Team provided for our stories so we could be unburdened with what is only temporary and focus on our eternal destiny."

The evening was a perfect balance between personal attention and corporate unity. Before Garrick released the group back to their life outside the museum, he read from one of his many favorite books, Isaiah. "I'm so taken with the presence of the Trinity. I am blessed to offer this gift to everyone. I am here to fix broken hearts and broken bodies. Issues and people do not hold you captive. Everything that matters is here." It was almost too much to comprehend. They had just listened to the anointed Word resonating from the lips of the Beloved. They each received the blessing deeply. They would savor and remember this moment. The air was still. Their hearts had been penetrated.

The Owner looked at each one of them individually and then at the group collectively. He knew every page of their lives, and he knew their hearts and had shown them His. They trembled as He called their names. "Adlai, Colson, Rhesa, Matthew, Ragan, Miron, Peter, bravo! I'm so proud of these seven, each a masterpiece. You are chosen. Take with you our blessing, our heart, and our presence."

Someday we will have time to tour every room and applaud every unparalleled novel, of those who had decades to be archived and those who were never born. The collection is almost finished, and the dedication is approaching. The expressions are everywhere.

"His team was present, and as anticipated, He announced, 'This is it! This will be the last biography. After all of these years working together, we're so close to accomplishing this dream. We'll interview for and edit and place on the shelf just one more biography before the dedication we've been longing to experience together.'"

Whether you have reservations or not, the room is there desiring to be unlocked. There's just one more room to open, one more life to redeem. There's a bookcase to build, a season to restore. There's a shelf to complete, a year to fulfill. There's one empty place on the shelf, one more month to dream. There's a chapter to write, a week to minister. There's a page to type, a day to love. There's a paragraph under construction, an hour to pray. There's a sentence to finish, a minute to believe. There's just one more word to utter, a moment to hope.

There's time and space for just one more. The collection is still missing something, one word or an entire room. There's still one last opportunity to do something special with the time remaining, and the Team isn't willing to undergo the dedication, despite the current status of the world, until it is realized. If you were the only soul, it was worth it all.

Journal

The Source

It's natural to question fictional interpretation. In developing the characters of the team, the sources were checked. All the references are contained in the Guidebook written years ago for future staff, the Book that helped Rhesa sleep, know mankind and herself and their Designer, and find closure. The Bible applies to everything. The answer to every form of research dilemma is already there. It is prevalent and relevant.

If you prefer the search and the study or if you simply want the information provided, the next chapter contains the correlations. Either way, you will probably have some new ones revealed. All are welcome. You're invited to see if there are not more interpretations while exploring these character traits. To share the discovery fuels more discovery.

Appendix A gives a comprehensive but not exhaustive list of references in the Bible to the Spirit. Appendix B is an alphabetical list of traits of the Spirit obtained from the Biblical references. Appendix C is the corresponding text from this book, in random order. Appendix D is characters and reference numbers, for concentration on a favorite character or hint towards a particular passage. Appendix E is locations in the book for context. A read without the use of any appendix offers the greatest challenge. A cross-reference of all five is the least time-consuming and the better option for those not into page-turning, Appendix F. Appendix G is the answers for Appendix B when compared to Appendix A, and Appendix H is the answers for Appendix C when compared to Appendix A. None of the above, all of the above, or any combination thereof, it's reader's choice. After all, the book was written for you.

Appendices A through E are labeled in this example from Appendix F:

42-44) <u>A</u> John 14:26 But the Comforter, which is the Holy Ghost, whom the Father will send in my name, he shall teach you all things, and bring all things to your remembrance, whatsoever I have said unto you. (<u>B</u> Comforts, Teaches, Reminds)

<u>C</u> Kecia and Aaron immediately were part of the organization. Each provided multiple skills and took on several roles and had a quality that seemed incomprehensible. Kecia had a presence about her that granted a place of solace. Aaron's gifts included thorough instruction and the ability to prompt a memory and direct it to the answer. (<u>D</u> Team) <u>E</u> page 8

There's additionally countless other references to something nonfiction, snippets of text that may remind you of something else. The "poetic composition" Aaron was known for is a reference to the ability of the Spirit to bring to our mind Scripture as a tool in our lives. It appeared that Colson was referring to a founding father writing in the "Constitution" that all men are created equal. He was not. Every moment we experience, whether awake or asleep, it's abundant, and we can invite the disclosure.

There are threads of similar traits in this list of references, and an array of complex qualities too difficult to fully understand, but many times the Spirit's role is to fill. Without fail, we can go to this resource when we feel hollow and shallow and empty. We can become so saturated with this source and all of the good that naturally flows from it that there just is not room for anything else.

Space is provided in Appendix F to note insights adjacent to the Biblical passages and to reconstruct the fictional text with personal impressions and words, if desired.

Appendices

Appendix A: References

1-2) Genesis 1:2 And the earth was without form, and void; and darkness was upon the face of the deep. And the Spirit of God moved upon the face of the waters.

3-4) Genesis 6:3 And the Lord said, My Spirit shall not always strive with man, for that he also is flesh.

5-6) Exodus 31:3 And I have filled him with the Spirit of God, in wisdom, and in understanding, and in knowledge, and in all manner of workmanship.

7) Job 33:4 The Spirit of God hath made me, and the breath of the Almighty hath given me life.

8-9) Psalm 51:11-12 Cast me not away from thy presence; and take not thy Holy Spirit from me.

Restore unto me the joy of thy salvation; and uphold me with thy free Spirit.

10-13) Psalm 139:7-13 Whither shall I go from thy Spirit? Or whither shall I flee from thy presence?

If I ascend up into heaven, thou art there: if I make my bed in hell, behold, thou art there.

If I take the wings of the morning, and dwell in the uttermost parts of the sea;

even there shall thy hand lead me, and thy right hand shall hold me.

If I say, Surely the darkness shall cover me; even the night shall be light about me.

Yea, the darkness hideth not from thee; but the night shineth as the day; the darkness and the light are both alike to thee.

For thou hast possessed my reins: thou hast covered me in my mother's womb.

14) Isaiah 32:15 Until the Spirit be poured upon us from on high, and the wilderness be fruitful field, and the fruitful field be counted for a forest.

15-16) Isaiah 40:13-14 Who hath directed the Spirit of the Lord, or being his counselor hath taught him?

With whom took he counsel, and who instructed him, and taught him in the path of judgment, and taught him knowledge, and showed to him the way of understanding?

17-18) Isaiah 61:1-3 The Spirit of the Lord God is upon me; because the Lord hath anointed me to preach good tidings unto the meek; he hath sent me to bind up the brokenhearted, to proclaim liberty to the captives, and the opening of the prison to them that are bound;

To proclaim the acceptable year of the Lord, and the day of vengeance of our God; to comfort all that mourn;

To appoint unto them that mourn in Zion, to give unto them beauty for ashes, the oil of joy for mourning, the garment of praise for the spirit of heaviness; that they might be called trees of righteousness, the planting of the Lord, that he might be glorified.

19) Isaiah 63:10 But they rebelled, and vexed his Holy Spirit: therefore he was turned to be their enemy, and he fought against them.

20-21) Joel 2:28-29, Acts 2:17-18 And it shall come to pass afterward, that I will pour out my Spirit upon all flesh;

and your sons and your daughters shall prophecy, your old men shall dream dreams, your young men shall see visions:

And also upon the servants and upon the handmaids in those days will I pour out my Spirit.

22) Micah 3:8 But truly I am full of power by the Spirit of the Lord, and of judgment, and of might, to declare unto Jacob his transgression, and to Israel his sin.

23-24) Zechariah 12:10 And I will pour upon the house of David, and upon the inhabitants of Jerusalem, the Spirit of grace and of supplications.

25) Matthew 3:16 And Jesus, when he was baptized, went up straightway out of the water: and, lo, the heavens were opened unto him, and he saw the Spirit of God descending like a dove, and lighting upon him.

26) Matthew 10:20 For it is not ye that speak but the Spirit of your Father which speaketh in you.

27) Matthew 12:28 But if I cast out devils by the Spirit of God, then the kingdom of God is come unto you.

28) Matthew 12:31-32 Wherefore I say unto you, all manner of sin and blasphemy shall be forgiven unto men: but the blasphemy against the Holy Ghost shall not be forgiven unto men.

And whosoever speaketh a word against the Son of Man, it shall be forgiven him: but whosoever speaketh against the Holy Ghost, it shall not be forgiven him, neither in this world, neither in the world to come.

29) Matthew 28:19 Go ye therefore and teach all nations, baptizing them in the name of the Father, and of the Son, and of the Holy Ghost.

30) Luke 1:15 For he shall be great in the sight of the Lord, and shall drink neither wine nor strong drink; and he shall be filled with the Holy Ghost, even from his mother's womb.

31) Luke 1:35 And the angel answered and said unto her, The Holy Ghost shall come upon thee, and the power of the Highest shall overshadow thee: therefore also that holy thing which shall be born of thee shall be called the Son of God.

32) Luke 1:41 And it came to pass, when Elizabeth heard the salutation of Mary, the babe leaped in her womb; and Elizabeth was filled with the Holy Ghost.

33) Luke 1:67 And his father Zechariah was filled with the Holy Ghost, and prophesied, saying.

34) Luke 4:1 And Jesus being full of the Holy Ghost returned from Jordan, and was led by the Spirit into the wilderness.

35) Luke 4:17-19 And there was delivered unto him the book of the prophet Isaiah. And when he had opened the book, he found the place where it was written,

The Spirit of the Lord is upon me, because he hath anointed me to preach the gospel to the poor; he hath sent me to heal the broken-hearted, to preach deliverance to the captives, and recovering of sight to the blind, to set at liberty them that are bruised,

to preach the acceptable year of the Lord.

36-37) John 3:5-8 Jesus answered, verily, verily, I say unto thee, except a man be born of water and of the Spirit, he cannot enter into the kingdom of God.

That which is born of the flesh is flesh; and that which is born of the Spirit is Spirit.

Marvel not that I said unto thee, ye must be born again.

The wind bloweth where it listeth, and thou hearest the sound thereof, but canst not tell whence it cometh, and whither it goeth: so is every one that is born of the Spirit.

38-39) John 7:38-39 He that believeth on me, as the Scripture hath said, out of his belly shall flow rivers of living waters.

But this spake he of the Spirit, which they that believe on him should receive: for the Holy Ghost was not yet given; because that Jesus was not yet glorified.

40-41) John 14:16-18 And I will pray the Father, and he shall give you another Comforter, that he may abide with you forever;

Even the Spirit of truth, whom the world cannot receive, because it seeth him not, neither knoweth him, but ye know him for he dwelleth with you, and shall be in you.

I will not leave you comfortless: I will come to you.

42-44) John 14:26 But the Comforter, which is the Holy Ghost, whom the Father will send in my name, he shall teach you all things, and bring all things to your remembrance, whatsoever I have said unto you.

45-50) John 16:7-15 Nevertheless I tell you the truth; it is expedient for you that I go away: for if I go not away, the Comforter will not come unto you; but if I depart, I will send him unto you.

And when he is come, he will reprove the world of sin, and of righteousness, and of judgment:

Of sin, because they believe not on me;

Of righteousness, because I go to my Father, and ye see me no more;

Of judgment, because the prince of this world is judged.

I have yet many things to say unto you, but ye cannot bear them now.

Howbeit when he, the Spirit of truth, is come, he will guide you into all truth: for he shall not speak of himself, but whatsoever he shall hear, that shall he speak; and he will show you things to come.

He shall glorify me: for he shall receive of mine, and shall show it unto you.

All things that the Father hath are mine: therefore said I, that he shall take of mine, and shall show it unto you.

51) Acts 1:16 Men and brethren, this Scripture must needs have been fulfilled, which the Holy Ghost by the mouth of David spake before concerning Judas, which was guide to them that took Jesus.

52) Acts 2:4 And they were all filled with the Holy Ghost, and began to speak with other tongues, as the Spirit gave them utterance.

53) Acts 2:33 Therefore being by the right hand of God exalted, and having received of the Father the promise of the Holy Ghost, he hath shed forth this, which ye now see and hear.

54) Acts 2:38 Then Peter said unto them, repent, and be baptized every one of you in the name of Jesus Christ for the remission of sins, and ye shall receive the gift of the Holy Ghost.

55) Acts 4:8 Then Peter, filled with the Holy Ghost, said unto them, ye rulers of the people, and elders of Israel.

56) Acts 5:3-4 But Peter said, Ananias, why hath Satan filled thine heart to lie to the Holy Ghost, and to keep back part of the price of the land? While it remained, was it not thine own? And after it was sold, was it not in thine own power? Why has thou conceived this thing in thine heart? Thou hast not lied unto men but unto God.

57-58) Acts 5:32 And we are his witnesses of these things; and so is also the Holy Ghost, whom God hath given to them that obey him.

59-61) Acts 6:3-5 Wherefore, brethren, look ye out among you seven men of honest report, full of the Holy Ghost and wisdom, whom we may appoint over this business.

But we will give ourselves continually to prayer, and to the ministry of the word.

And the saying pleased the whole multitude: and they chose Stephen, a man full of faith and of the Holy Ghost, and Philip, and Prochorus, and Nicanor, and Timon, and Parmenas, and Nicolas a proselyte of Antioch.

62) Acts 7:51 Ye stiffnecked and uncircumcised in heart and ears, ye do always resist the Holy Ghost: as your fathers did, so do ye.

63) Acts 7:55 But he, being full of the Holy Ghost, looked up steadfastly into heaven, and saw the glory of God, and Jesus standing on the right hand of God.

64) Acts 8:29 Then the Spirit said unto Philip, go near, and join thyself to this chariot.

65) Acts 9:31 Then had the churches rest throughout all Judea and Galilee and Samaria, and were edified; and walking in the fear of the Lord, and in the comfort of the Holy Ghost, were multiplied.

66) Acts 10:45 And they of the circumcision which believed were astonished, as many as came with Peter, because that on the Gentiles also was poured out the gift of the Holy Ghost.

67) Acts 11:24 For he was a good man, and full of the Holy Ghost and of faith: and much people was added unto the Lord.

68) Acts 13:2-4 As they ministered to the Lord, and fasted, the Holy Ghost said, separate me Barnabas and Saul for the work whereunto I have called them.

And when they had fasted and prayed, and laid their hands on them, they sent them away.

So they, being sent forth by the Holy Ghost, departed unto Seleucia, and from then they sailed to Cyprus.

69) Acts 13:9 Then Saul, [who also is called Paul,] filled with the Holy Ghost, set his eyes on him.

70) Acts 13:52 And the disciples were filled with joy, and with the Holy Ghost.

71) Acts 20:22-23 And now, behold, I go bound in the spirit unto Jerusalem, not knowing the things that shall befall me there:

Save that the Holy Ghost witnesseth in every city, saying that bonds and afflictions abide me.

72) Acts 20:28 Take heed thereof unto yourselves, and to all the flock, over the which the Holy Ghost hath made you overseers, to feed the church of God, which he hath purchased with his own blood.

73) Acts 28:25 And when they agreed not among themselves, they departed, after that Paul had spoken one word, Well spake the Holy Ghost by Isaiah the prophet unto our fathers.

74) Romans 1:4 And declared to be the Son of God with power, according to the Spirit of holiness, by the resurrection from the dead.

75) Romans 8:2 For the law of the Spirit of life in Christ Jesus hath made me free from the law of sin and death.

76-77) Romans 8:9 But ye are not in the flesh, but in the Spirit, if so be that the Spirit of God dwell in you. Now if any man have not the Spirit of Christ, he is none of his.

78-79) Romans 8:11 But if the Spirit of him that raised up Jesus from the dead dwell in you, he that raised up Christ from the dead shall also quicken your mortal bodies by his Spirit that dwelleth in you.

80-83) Romans 8:13-16 For if ye live after the flesh, ye shall die: but if ye through the Spirit do mortify the deeds of the body, ye shall live.

For as many as are led by the Spirit of God, they are the sons of God.

For ye have not received the spirit of bondage again to fear; but ye have received the Spirit of adoption, whereby we cry, Abba, Father.

The Spirit itself beareth witness with our spirit, that we are the children of God.

84-85) Romans 8:26 Likewise the Spirit also helpeth our infirmities: for we know not what we should pray for as we ought: but the Spirit itself maketh intercession for us with groanings which cannot be uttered.

86) Romans 14:17 For the kingdom of God is not meat and drink; but righteousness, and peace, and joy in the Holy Ghost.

87) Romans 15:16 That I should be the minister of Jesus Christ to the Gentiles, ministering the gospel of God, that the offering up of the Gentiles might be acceptable, being sanctified by the Holy Ghost.

88-93) 1 Corinthians 2:10-14 But God hath revealed them unto us by his Spirit: for the Spirit searcheth all things, yea, the deep things of God.

For what man knoweth the things of a man, save the spirit of man which is in him? Even so the things of God knoweth no man, but the Spirit of God.

Now we have received, not the spirit of the world, but the Spirit which is of God; that we might know the things that are freely given to us of God.

Which things also we speak, not in the words which man's wisdom teacheth, but which the Holy Ghost teacheth; comparing spiritual things with spiritual.

But the natural man receiveth not the things of the Spirit of God: for they are foolishness unto him: neither can he know them, because they are spiritually discerned.

94-99) I Corinthians 12:3-13 Wherefore I give you to understand, that no man speaking by the Spirit of God calleth Jesus accursed: and that no man can say that Jesus is the Lord, but by the Holy Ghost.

Now there are diversities of gifts, but the same Spirit.

And there are differences of administrations, but the same Lord.

And there are diversities of operations, but it is the same God which worketh all in all.

But the manifestation of the Spirit is given to every man to profit withal.

For to one is given by the Spirit the word of wisdom; to another the word of knowledge by the same Spirit;

To another faith by the same Spirit; to another the gifts of healing by the same Spirit;

To another the working of miracles; to another prophecy; to another discerning of spirits; to another divers kinds of tongues; to another the interpretation of tongues:

But all these worketh that one and the selfsame Spirit, dividing to every man severally as he will.

For as the body is one, and hath many members, and all the members of that one body, being many, are one body: so also is Christ.

For by one Spirit are we all baptized into one body, whether we be Jews or Gentiles, whether we be bond or free; and have been all made to drink into one Spirit.

100) 2 Corinthians 13:14 The grace of the Lord Jesus Christ and the love of God, and the communion of the Holy Ghost, be with you all. Amen.

101) Galatians 4:6 And because ye are sons, God hath sent forth the Spirit of his Son into your hearts, crying, Abba, Father.

102-103) Galatians 5:16-18 This I say then, Walk in the Spirit, and ye shall not fulfill the lust of the flesh.

For the flesh lusteth against the Spirit, and the Spirit against the flesh: and these are contrary the one to the other: so that ye cannot do the things that ye would.

But if ye be led of the Spirit, ye are not under the law.

104) Galatians 5:22-23 But the fruit of the Spirit is love, joy, peace, long-suffering, gentleness, goodness, faith, meekness, temperance: against such there is no law.

105) Ephesians 1:17 That the God of our Lord Jesus Christ, the Father of glory, may give unto you the Spirit of wisdom and revelation in the knowledge of him.

106) Ephesians 3:16 That he would grant you, according to the riches of his glory, to be strengthened with might by his Spirit in the inner man.

107) Ephesians 4:30 And grieve not the holy Spirit of God, whereby ye are sealed unto the day of redemption.

108) Ephesians 6:17 And take the helmet of salvation, and the sword of the Spirit, which is the word of God.

109) 2 Thessalonians 2:13 But we are bound to give thanks always to God for you, brethren beloved of the Lord, because God hath from the beginning chosen you to salvation through sanctification of the Spirit and belief of the truth.

110) 1 Timothy 3:16 And without controversy great is the mystery of godliness: God was manifest in the flesh, justified in the Spirit, seen of angels, preached unto the Gentiles, believed on in the world, received up into glory.

111) Hebrews 9:14 How much more shall the blood of Christ, who through the eternal Spirit offered himself without spot to God, purge your conscience from dead works to serve the living God?

112) Hebrews 10:15 Whereof the Holy Ghost also is a witness to us: for after that he had said before.

113) 1 Peter 4:14 If ye be reproached for the name of Christ, happy are ye; for the Spirit of glory and of God resteth upon you.

114) 1 John 2:20, 27 But ye have an unction from the Holy One, and ye know all things.

But the anointing which ye have received of him abideth in you, and ye need not that any man teach you: but as the same anointing teacheth you of all things, and is truth, and is no lie, and even as it hath taught you, ye shall abide in him.

115) 1 John 4:1-6 Beloved, believe not every spirit, but try the spirits whether they are of God: because many false prophets are gone out into the world.

Hereby know ye the Spirit of God: every spirit that confesseth that Jesus Christ is come in the flesh is of God:

and every spirit that confesseth not that Jesus Christ is come in the flesh is not of God: and this is that spirit of anti-christ, whereof ye have heard that it should come; and even now already is it in the world.

Ye are of God, little children, and have overcome them: because greater is he that is in you, than he that is in the world.

They are of the world: therefore speak they of the world, and the world heareth them.

We are of God: he that knoweth God heareth us: he that is not of God heareth not us.

Hereby know we the Spirit of truth, and the spirit of error.

116) Revelation 19:10 And I fell at his feet to worship him. And he said unto me, See thou do it not: I am thy fellow servant, and of thy brethren that have the testimony of Jesus: worship God: for the testimony of Jesus is the Spirit of prophecy.

Appendix B: Traits

001) _____   Accompanies

002) _____   Adopts

003) _____   Affirms the Creator

004) _____   Aligns

005) _____   Anoints

006) _____   Anoints

007) _____   Apportions

008) _____   Arrives

009) _____   Atones

010) _____   Bears fruit

011) _____   Bears witness

012) _____   Belongs with God

013) _____   Bestows

014) _____   Cherished

015) _____   Chooses leaders

016) _____   Comfort

017) _____   Comforts

018) _____   Comforts

019) _____   Commissions

020) _____   Communes

021) _____   Connects

022) _____   Convinces

023) _____   Creates

024) _____   Creation

025) _____   Design

026) _____   Directs

027) _____   Displays

028) _____   Education

029) _____   Empowers

030) _____	Engages
031) _____	Enlightens
032) _____	Eternal consequences for sinning against
033) _____	Explores
034) _____	Faith
035) _____	Fills
036) _____	Fills
037) _____	Fills
038) _____	Fills
039) _____	Fills
040) _____	Fills
041) _____	Fills
042) _____	Fills
043) _____	Fills
044) _____	Fills
045) _____	Frees
046) _____	Gift to the obedient
047) _____	Given to earth
048) _____	Given to everyone
049) _____	Gives
050) _____	Gives discernment
051) _____	Gives discernment
052) _____	Glorifies
053) _____	Grieved
054) _____	Guidance
055) _____	Guides
056) _____	Helps our infirmities
057) _____	Holy
058) _____	Honest reputation
059) _____	Honors
060) _____	Indwells
061) _____	Informs

062) _____	Inspirational
063) _____	Intercedes
064) _____	Judgment
065) _____	Justifies
066) _____	Leads descendants
067) _____	Life-giving
068) _____	Mysterious
069) _____	Nature
070) _____	Nondiscriminatory
071) _____	Offers righteousness, peace, and joy
072) _____	Omnipotent
073) _____	Omnipresence
074) _____	Omniscient
075) _____	One with God
076) _____	Performs miracles
077) _____	Prohibits
078) _____	Promised
079) _____	Prophesies Jesus
080) _____	Provides for prayer
081) _____	Provides for unmerited favor
082) _____	Radiance
083) _____	Received upon faith
084) _____	Reminds
085) _____	Resisted
086) _____	Restorative
087) _____	Restores
088) _____	Restrains and releases
089) _____	Resurrects
090) _____	Reveals
091) _____	Reveals
092) _____	Sanctifies
093) _____	Simplifies

094) _____ Skill
095) _____ Speaks
096) _____ Speaks through people
097) _____ Speaks through people
098) _____ Speaks through prophets
099) _____ Strengthens
100) _____ Subdues
101) _____ Sustains
102) _____ Teaches
103) _____ Teaches
104) _____ Transforms
105) _____ Trinity
106) _____ Truth
107) _____ Unburdens
108) _____ Upholds
109) _____ Uses everything for good
110) _____ Virtuous
111) _____ Willing
112) _____ Wisdom
113) _____ Wisdom
114) _____ Witness
115) _____ Witnesses
116) _____ Witnesses

Appendix C: Text

_____1-2) If she focused on the truth, she could let things go that are harmful yet somehow are also compelling. A lie evokes this emotion, and evil can be alluring still when good is right next to it. It's debilitating. When reality wins, restrictions aren't necessary.

_____3) Miron knew every life was composed with complete inspiration and brilliance, including his.

_____4-5) The archivist in him was so concerned with the preservation of the collection, he talked to the owner about employing staff who would take great care with the truth for each piece. They would provide support and stay with the story ad infinitum. Manipulation of facts had become so prevalent, it was hard to recognize sincerity. Garrick's work could be trusted to be without embellishment. It didn't need it. It was important that he provide that reassurance through personnel.

_____6) Kecia took the time to help Peter see how something that he hoped was just okay had become something good and would continue to grow.

_____7) Colson often saw in the smallest creature the opportunity for something larger than life.

_____8-11) The locations where staff would find themselves were endless, and they had amazing adventures pursuing their assignment. They were present for the highs and the lows in the process. Spontaneous long distance and difficult travel did not shake their resolve to conduct the interview and effectively support the participant. When negativity crept in, they could deal with it. They had an integral part in these lives.

_____12) She had a grasp on the situation but received so much defiance and friction, there was no opportunity to talk about all of the people he was negatively affecting with his take-over.

_____13) Simply being near her generated a festive mood.

_____14) "Take with you our blessing, our heart, and our presence."

_____15) "It doesn't matter, if it's for the right reason. The outcome is actually positive. It will be obvious who's on your side."

_____16) No one was immune from the impact of the staff, regardless of their station in life.

_____17) "Matthew could predict with certainty that whether the letter was sent to you by his commanding officer or he returned and gifted it to someone who desperately needed hope, its purpose was far-reaching."

When Rhesa announced the direction of her future with such confidence, Kecia understood the encounter she had had.

After returning home, Peter experienced something he had not in years. Whether awake or resting, a new dream was taking place in his soul.

For Colson, the lens provided so much more than pictures and images. It was a gift of vision to him. He could see how things used to be and should be and will be.

_____18) Dad, I know there are many industries that promote this tough language, and obviously in my youth I would not have been able to hold back my words, but now I feel liberated to speak only my faith.

_____19) The staff had selected gifts unique to each one of them. This would assist them in their distinct service for the team. The owner would accomplish awesome plans in and through their lives.

_____20) Staff would assure their days would be so rich that everyone around them would benefit as well.

_____21) "Your gift is insight. It will guide your heart and change your life."

Aaron instructed his student once again, "Your gift is not limited to a single course of study. Your philosophy will be broad and extensive and will carry you through difficult decisions."

The symbol was given to him by his parents, but it was the spirit who gave him the gift of faith.

"Your gift is healing. You've been honored to experience some of the pain of the editor and understand how even the most remote parts of the body die without a constant flow of blood. Though this season has felt like repetitive injury to your body and soul, there is redemptive healing through the spirit."

"You will see miracles all around you and be involved in their spectacle."

"This now becomes your symbol, and your gift is speech. You have a story to tell in a manner that will be received."

"Your gift is intuition. You will distinguish between truth and deception."

Kecia stated, "Love is the symbol. Your gift is language, and Amy will facilitate."

_____22) Kecia and Aaron entrusted all these attributes to these souls they had followed intently.

_____23) Kecia told her she was thinking about how much Garrick adores this stuff, the fact that all of these individuals came from separate circumstances and are now here together learning about each other and how their paths have crossed.

_____24) "Every parent desires that their child be gifted with incredible, unending courage that completely envelops who they are."

_____25) Often when Adlai couldn't find words to say how she was feeling, she repeated some of the things Kecia had told her.

_____26-27) Colson soaked up everything Aaron poured. He learned the history of the cameras and understood how they worked and knew what lighting was appropriate and why. His hands were steady and his eyes keen.

_____28) This process of studying deeply the reality of the past, with the guidance of Kecia, brought Peter an overwhelming sense of clarity and ability to address his industry in particular and business as a whole.

_____29) The owner, editor, and staff were solidly cohesive.

_____30-31) Adlai hoped she would never move away. She loved herself from A to Z when she was with Kecia, who gladly supported her adventures. Many evenings she would arrive at Kecia's home to play their favorite game of "Well, why not?"

_____32-33) With all his gifts and characteristics, at the core Aaron was an educator. His fellow teachers would often come to him when they had questions themselves. His advice was always directed toward what is right and just. He'd find a way to help them grasp the concept at hand.

_____34) Something that seemed impossible to everyone, they could orchestrate.

_____35-36) Kecia and Aaron knew if they became a part of these lives, they would have the same life-restoring impact they had once had with Garrick.

_____37) Kecia told her to reflect on her thoughts and circumstances and they would talk about it at their next dinner.

_____38) Garrick was delighted to be with Kecia and Aaron as they transitioned into this phase. They were with him at a critical juncture.

_____39) They were all so enamored with the gift that had been given to them, they knew they would never look or sound the same again.

_____40) This encounter changed their direction. Each of them would find themselves in a place of influence with the ability to care for others who also had been captured by the author's love.

_____41) "Matthew just seemed saturated with good."

_____42) "The editor is the owner's son, and you are the owner's children as well. He sent us to be with you. The owner is your author, but you may also address him as dad."

_____43-45) Kecia and Aaron immediately were part of the organization. Each provided multiple skills and took on several roles and had a quality that seemed incomprehensible. Kecia had a presence about her that granted a place of solace. Aaron's gifts included thorough instruction and the ability to prompt a memory and direct it to the answer.

_____46-47) Kecia was all about the stuff that lasts. She had a way with life and rubbed off on everyone around her, with this uncanny ability to flit in and out of lives at the right time.

_____48) It wasn't the choice of topic but the choice of human behavior that caused Kecia to be so visibly bothered.

_____49) Too much of his life had been spent toiling when goodness and rest and great happiness is so readily available.

_____50) Before Garrick released the group back to their life outside the museum, he read from one of his many favorite books, Isaiah. "I'm so taken with the presence of the Trinity. I am blessed to offer this gift to everyone. I am here to fix broken hearts and broken bodies. Issues and people do not hold you captive. Everything that matters is here."

_____51) With more support in the field and Garrick as editor, the staff was an incredible reflection of his strength.

_____52) When Kecia said with confidence that everything wrong hinges on lack of faith, her words pierced Ragan. How could she establish so much in such a non-condemning way?

Kecia was very persuasive, but she truly won Rhesa over to the idea when she said, "With the writing and editing, how could this story not have merit? Not to mention the facilities and resources and business model and countless hours from the dedicated team members."

Ragan could spend the whole evening with her and not hear one critical, judgmental remark. When she asked her how she had acquired this skill, Kecia responded, "The best of us is judged. The rest don't need to be."

_____53) Just her presence brought out Peter's ability to see the truth.

_____54) Adlai glowed when Kecia told her that these words came directly from the owner of the museum.

_____55) "Kecia and Aaron have given you a glimpse into something that you long for, heaven."

_____56) They drew upon his character and represented him well. The reputation of the owner naturally flowed to the editor.

_____57) When she felt empty, Ragan remembered Kecia telling her that her faith was the source of constant, overflowing life.

_____58) The plan had been in place for years, but when the timing was right, Garrick spoke to his colleagues about additional personnel. He then could be promoted to editor.

_____59) Access to staff was simple because of the work already done by the editor.

_____60) "He stated that he was drawn to this mission even without knowing what it would entail. I affirmed to him that it would be difficult."

_____61) She recognized the miracle of the darkness that was gone after one of the most intense evenings she and Kecia had spent together.

_____62-63) Rhesa sat and looked deep into the tide and wondered where the starting point was and how long it took to reach this side.

_____64) Colson was determined to follow Aaron's example and be known for his integrity at the purest level.

_____65) Ragan's understanding of people and the intricacies of life grew every time she listened to Kecia.

_____66) It would be easy for Adlai to believe in the incredible universe, especially after taking in everything Kecia had to show her.

_____67) "Aaron and Kecia have been your teacher and comforter, but they are not just for a chosen few, nor are they given to the spiritually elite, whether self-defined or by the world's standards. The spirit is for all mankind."

_____68-69) She felt strong enough to reach out to others who were suffering. It had been long enough. She could now grieve with them and help them find a harvest in the embers that would only make them stronger and validate the purpose of it all.

_____70) Listening to Kecia talk about principles caused Ragan to be in a place where she had never been. It was this strange mix of being a child learning for the first time and soaking it all in to a maturity level well beyond yesterday.

_____71) The staff explained they all had been selected not just for an adventure or even a season of personal growth but for a lifetime of worship. The tasks they would undertake in their daily lives, whether joyous or heavy, and the relationships they would nurture would bless the team. They were not dismissed from the Jenski; they were appointed by the spirit.

_____72) The message Aaron portrayed was powerful, and it came out clearly through Matthew's words.

_____73) They would speak always about the incredible artistry the editor would bring to a story.

_____74) Kecia believed that ministers conveyed the message to those who needed it.

_____75) In all their work, the title of staff commanded the same respect as that of the owner.

_____76) "He had a pure heart and was never empty when it came to his convictions. His faith was contagious."

_____77) It is all completely liberating.

_____78) He wondered what he ever could have done to deserve the hours Aaron spent pouring into his life and found himself wanting to do the same for others.

_____79) Ragan was mesmerized listening to her pray and found her own prayers transformed in her presence.

_____80) Peter was replete with the ideology he and Kecia had discussed as he confronted the owner of the company that solicited his competitor.

_____81) She now had the tenacity and vision to change her definition of life.

_____82) He told them all that they had been compelled by his spirit to be there because they already belonged.

_____83) "This will not enslave me or consume me. I've been embraced by my father."

_____84) "It will be infinitely visible to you through this experience that you are my very own."

_____85) "Your lives are treasured because you have always belonged here with us. Your membership has been donated and your trust in the organization acknowledged."

_____86) She was too excited to wait to share details of the incredible day they would travel to the Jenski Museum with the rest of the group to experience history in the making.

_____87) Kecia had pursued every morsel of information to the finest detail that the owner had in place. She did so in order to impart this to everyone.

_____88) The staff knew everything there was to know about the owner, his dreams and intentions and vision.

_____89) "You're too smart to fill your head with that noise. You need time without the clutter to listen to nothing but the wind and understand how rich your life is."

_____90) I know it may not seem logical for me to think this way, and I understand how this might encourage criticism. This isn't from a textbook, protocol, or guideline, but I've learned to listen to a source that is scholarly and unlike anything I've ever known.

_____91) Her ability to perceive beyond the obvious and ordinary matured as they spent time together exploring every topic important to them.

_____92) Colson was completely lost in their expression of love, was stable in his gaze but trembled too much to photograph anything when he saw the Jenski he had heard so much about, its brilliant owner, and his trusted editor standing next to him, both anxiously waiting to welcome everyone.

_____93) "There are things you should question. A lot of people try to claim something is virtuous when it's their own agenda they are trying to promote. Bottom line, it shouldn't conflict with your faith, but there's a destructive mindset out there that I believe will get worse. That's all in the past for you.

You have something greater now. It's substance over fluff, certainty over fallacy."

_____94) He ushered in a sense of hope for the future.

_____95) "Your lives have been perfectly edited by my son and completely refined by my spirit."

_____96) Part of the result of all this for Rhesa was a new definition of love. All she could do was display it because she sure couldn't explain it.

If you could somehow test it on a happiness meter, the cheerfulness left in her wake was off the chart.

At even the slightest glance, the contentment that had been missing so long in his life was clearly evident on Peter's face.

Miron was in it for the long haul.

As lively as Adlai was, she could also be very gentle.

Colson was just a good kid.

"Matthew believed with every fiber in him that this was ultimately what he was to do with the rest of his life."

Aaron's character served him well in this role. He quietly went about his work without unnecessary confrontation or a combative attitude.

Kecia saw great hope in a newfound ability to let things go that used to gnaw at her. There was no rule that said she had to carry that load.

_____97) I have listened intently to the reverence in speaking of the Beloved Soldier.

_____98) Since Garrick was in his ultimate role and now physically located at the museum, he had the owner's blessing to send the staff to the field.

_____99) I want to live without regret, knowing that I am accountable only to the one who calls my name at the rescue mission that counts.

_____100) She was enjoying a lot of still rather new freedoms. Matters she used to consider important were no longer when she truly searched her heart.

_____101) It was understood they were a package deal.

_____102) A sense of pride overwhelmed Aaron as he spoke. "I can attest to the change in Matthew."

_____103) "I know how hard you've tried to follow God's intention. Let me help you get through this."

_____104) I have every weapon I need in the eternal war of good over evil.

_____105-106) It was understood any staff with the museum is not associated with anything that may ultimately bring harm.

_____107) Miron spoke for all of the chosen when he stated, "We will always remember how the team provided for our stories so we could be unburdened with what is only temporary and focus on our eternal destiny."

_____108) Every place she touched became permeated with joy.

_____109) "You've been blessed, and your perception is good. This will remain with you. You don't have to look to other sources. This is your place of rest."

_____110) Even though he was very young, he had a spirit of authority about him.

_____111) Before meeting Kecia, for such a long time Rhesa felt nothing but alone. She now felt a part of something she still didn't fully understand, but it was encouraging, respectful, comforting, and fruitful.

_____112) Aaron explained that what had been done was unforgivable, and the outcome would be far-reaching.

_____113) When they relayed information, there was no doubting its validity. Their word was solid.

_____114) "This holiness is a conundrum. I know it's been taken care of for me, presented, affirmed and confirmed, taught and accepted, delivered."

_____115-116) "I don't know what to pray anymore. I know you've gone to bat for me. Words can't express the awesome advocate you are."

Appendix D: Characters, Reference numbers

Owner	56, 66, 81, 82, 83, 88, 89, 90
Editor	34, 39, 45, 49, 54, 77, 78, 79, 99, 116
Staff	3, 4, 10, 11, 12, 13, 20, 31, 34, 39, 45, 49, 52, 54, 56, 66, 70, 77, 78, 79, 81, 82, 83, 90, 96, 97, 98, 99, 112, 116
Team	29, 35, 40, 41, 42, 43, 44, 48, 50, 53, 63, 68, 72, 87, 95, 100, 101, 109, 111
Aaron	5, 6, 15, 16, 23, 28, 33, 51, 57, 58, 59, 71, 84, 85, 104
Kecia	8, 9, 14, 19, 21, 22, 24, 26, 27, 32, 36, 37, 38, 46, 47, 60, 61, 62, 64, 65, 69, 73, 80, 88, 89, 91, 93, 104, 105, 113, 114, 115
Adlai	8, 9, 26, 35, 48, 49, 52, 61, 63, 66, 68, 70, 72, 81, 83, 87, 88, 95, 96, 97, 98, 99, 100, 101, 104, 109, 111
Colson	5, 6, 21, 23, 25, 35, 49, 52, 59, 63, 66, 68, 70, 72, 81, 83, 87, 95, 96, 97, 98, 99, 100, 101, 104, 106, 109, 111
Matthew	21, 30, 35, 51, 52, 55, 57, 67, 68, 71, 72, 74, 75, 92, 94, 95, 96, 97, 98, 100, 104, 107, 108, 111
Matthew's parents	35, 49, 52, 63, 66, 68, 70, 72, 81, 83, 87, 95, 96, 97, 98, 99, 100, 101, 109, 111
Miron	7, 35, 49, 52, 58, 63, 66, 68, 70, 72, 81, 82, 83, 84, 85, 87, 95, 96, 97, 98, 99, 100, 101, 104, 109, 111

Peter	14, 21, 22, 35, 47, 49, 52, 63, 66, 68, 69, 70, 72, 81, 83, 86, 87, 95, 96, 97, 98, 99, 100, 101, 104, 109, 111
Amy	35, 49, 52, 63, 66, 68, 70, 72, 81, 83, 87, 95, 96, 97, 98, 99, 100, 101, 109, 111
Ragan	24, 27, 35, 38, 46, 49, 52, 60, 63, 64, 66, 68, 70, 72, 76, 80, 81, 83, 87, 93, 95, 96, 97, 98, 99, 100, 101, 102, 103, 104, 105, 109, 110, 111, 113, 115
Rhesa	1, 2, 17, 18, 21, 35, 46, 49, 52, 63, 65, 66, 68, 70, 72, 81, 83, 87, 91, 95, 96, 97, 98, 99, 100, 101, 104, 109, 111, 114

1-2	Rhesa
3-4	Staff
5-6	Aaron, Colson
7	Miron
8-9	Kecia, Adlai
10-13	Staff
14	Kecia, Peter
15-16	Aaron
17-18	Rhesa
19	Kecia
20	Staff
21	Kecia, Matthew, Rhesa, Peter, Colson
22	Kecia, Peter
23	Aaron, Colson
24	Kecia, Ragan
25	Colson
26	Kecia, Adlai
27	Kecia, Ragan
28	Aaron

29	Team
30	Matthew
31	Staff
32	Kecia
33	Aaron
34	Editor, Staff
35	Team, Adlai, Colson, Matthew, Matthew's parents, Miron, Peter and Amy, Ragan, Rhesa
36-37	Kecia
38	Kecia, Ragan
39	Editor, Staff
40-41	Team
42-44	Team
45	Editor, Staff
46	Kecia, Ragan, Rhesa
47	Kecia, Peter
48	Team, Adlai
49	Editor, Staff, Adlai, Colson, Matthew's parents, Miron, Peter and Amy, Ragan, Rhesa
50	Team
51	Aaron, Matthew
52	Staff, Adlai, Colson, Matthew, Matthew's parents, Miron, Peter and Amy, Ragan, Rhesa
53	Team
54	Editor, Staff
55	Matthew
56	Owner, Staff
57	Aaron, Matthew
58	Aaron, Miron
59	Aaron, Colson
60	Kecia, Ragan
61	Kecia, Adlai

62	Kecia
63	Team, Adlai, Colson, Matthew's parents, Miron, Peter and Amy, Ragan, Rhesa
64	Kecia, Ragan
65	Kecia, Rhesa
66	Owner, Staff, Adlai, Colson, Matthew's parents, Miron, Peter and Amy, Ragan, Rhesa
67	Matthew
68	Team, Adlai, Colson, Matthew, Matthew's parents, Miron, Peter and Amy, Ragan, Rhesa
69	Kecia, Peter
70	Staff, Adlai, Colson, Matthew's parents, Miron, Peter and Amy, Ragan, Rhesa
71	Aaron, Matthew
72	Team, Adlai, Colson, Matthew, Matthew's parents, Miron, Peter and Amy, Ragan, Rhesa
73	Kecia
74	Matthew
75	Matthew
76	Ragan
77	Editor, Staff
78-79	Editor, Staff
80	Kecia, Ragan
81	Owner, Staff, Adlai, Colson, Matthew's parents, Miron, Peter and Amy, Ragan, Rhesa
82	Owner, Staff, Miron
83	Owner, Staff, Adlai, Colson, Matthew's parents, Miron, Peter and Amy, Ragan, Rhesa
84-85	Aaron, Miron
86	Peter
87	Team, Adlai, Colson, Matthew's parents, Miron, Peter and Amy, Ragan, Rhesa

88	Owner, Kecia, Adlai
89	Owner, Kecia
90	Owner, Staff
91	Kecia, Rhesa
92	Matthew
93	Kecia, Ragan
94	Matthew
95	Team, Adlai, Colson, Matthew, Matthew's parents, Miron, Peter and Amy, Ragan, Rhesa
96	Staff, Adlai, Colson, Matthew, Matthew's parents, Miron, Peter and Amy, Ragan, Rhesa
97	Staff, Adlai, Colson, Matthew, Matthew's parents, Miron, Peter and Amy, Ragan, Rhesa
98	Staff, Adlai, Colson, Matthew, Matthew's parents, Miron, Peter and Amy, Ragan, Rhesa
99	Editor, Staff, Adlai, Colson, Matthew's parents, Miron, Peter and Amy, Ragan, Rhesa
100	Team, Adlai, Colson, Matthew, Matthew's parents, Miron, Peter and Amy, Ragan, Rhesa
101	Team, Adlai, Colson, Matthew's parents, Miron, Peter and Amy, Ragan, Rhesa
102-103	Ragan
104	Aaron, Kecia, Adlai, Colson, Matthew, Miron, Peter, Ragan, Rhesa
105	Kecia, Ragan
106	Colson
107	Matthew
108	Matthew
109	Team, Adlai, Colson, Matthew's parents, Miron, Peter and Amy, Ragan, Rhesa
110	Ragan

Appendix E: Page numbers

	Page
1-2)	83
3-4)	9
5-6)	61
7)	104
8-9)	35
10-13)	9
14)	30
15-16)	10
17-18)	87
19)	97
20-21)	9, 48, 87, 32, 60
22)	29
23-24)	73, 99
25)	60
26)	39
27)	99
28)	62
29)	8
30)	48
31)	8
32)	13
33)	9
34)	8
35)	142
36-37)	13
38-39)	92, 7
40-41)	7
42-44)	8

Appendix F: A through E

1-2) Genesis 1:2 And the earth was without form, and void; and darkness was upon the face of the deep. And the Spirit of God moved upon the face of the waters. (Creation, Nature)

Rhesa sat and looked deep into the tide and wondered where the starting point was and how long it took to reach this side. (Rhesa) page 83

3-4) Genesis 6:3 And the Lord said, My Spirit shall not always strive with man, for that he also is flesh. (Belongs with God, Virtuous)

It was understood any staff with the museum is not associated with anything that may ultimately bring harm. (Staff) page 9

5-6) Exodus 31:3 And I have filled him with the Spirit of God, in wisdom, and in understanding, and in knowledge, and in all manner of workmanship. (Wisdom, Skill)

Colson soaked up everything Aaron poured. He learned the history of the cameras and understood how they worked and knew what lighting was appropriate and why. His hands were steady and his eyes keen. (Aaron, Colson) page 61

7) Job 33:4 The Spirit of God hath made me, and the breath of the Almighty hath given me life. (Creates)

Miron knew every life was composed with complete inspiration and brilliance, including his. (Miron) page 104

8-9) Psalm 51:11-12 Cast me not away from thy presence; and take not thy Holy Spirit from me.
Restore unto me the joy of thy salvation; and uphold me with thy free Spirit. (Cherished, Willing)

Adlai hoped she would never move away. She loved herself from A to Z when she was with Kecia, who gladly supported her adventures. Many evenings she would arrive at Kecia's home to play their favorite game of "Well, why not?" (Kecia, Adlai)
page 35, 35

10-13) Psalm 139:7-13 Whither shall I go from thy Spirit? Or whither shall I flee from thy presence?
If I ascend up into heaven, thou art there: if I make my bed in hell, behold, thou art there.
If I take the wings of the morning, and dwell in the uttermost parts of the sea;
even there shall thy hand lead me, and thy right hand shall hold me.
If I say, Surely the darkness shall cover me; even the night shall be light about me.
Yea, the darkness hideth not from thee; but the night shineth as the day; the darkness and the light are both alike to thee.
For thou hast possessed my reins: thou hast covered me in my mother's womb. (Omnipresence, Guidance, Radiance, Design)

The locations where staff would find themselves were endless, and they had amazing adventures pursuing their assignment. They were present for the highs and the lows in the process. Spontaneous long distance and difficult travel did not shake their resolve to conduct the interview and effectively support the participant. When negativity crept in, they could deal with it. They had an integral part in these lives. (Staff) page 9

14) Isaiah 32:15 Until the Spirit be poured upon us from on high, and the wilderness be fruitful field, and the fruitful field be counted for a forest. (Restores)

Kecia took the time to help Peter see how something that he hoped was just okay had become something good and would continue to grow. (Kecia, Peter) page 30

15-16) Isaiah 40:13-14 Who hath directed the Spirit of the Lord, or being his counselor hath taught him?
With whom took he counsel, and who instructed him, and taught him in the path of judgment, and taught him knowledge, and showed to him the way of understanding? (Education, Judgment)

With all his gifts and characteristics, at the core Aaron was an educator. His fellow teachers would often come to him when they had questions themselves. His advice was always directed toward what is right and just. He'd find a way to help them grasp the concept at hand. (Aaron) page 10

17-18) Isaiah 61:1-3 The Spirit of the Lord God is upon me; because the Lord hath anointed me to preach good tidings unto the meek; he hath sent me to bind up the brokenhearted, to proclaim liberty to the captives, and the opening of the prison to them that are bound;
To proclaim the acceptable year of the Lord, and the day of vengeance of our God; to comfort all that mourn;
To appoint unto them that mourn in Zion, to give unto them beauty for ashes, the oil of joy for mourning, the garment of

praise for the spirit of heaviness; that they might be called trees of righteousness, the planting of the Lord, that he might be glorified. (Uses everything for good, Affirms the Creator)

She felt strong enough to reach out to others who were suffering. It had been long enough. She could now grieve with them and help them find a harvest in the embers that would only make them stronger and validate the purpose of it all. (Rhesa) page 87

19) Isaiah 63:10 But they rebelled, and vexed his Holy Spirit: therefore he was turned to be their enemy, and he fought against them. (Grieved)

It wasn't the choice of topic but the choice of human behavior that caused Kecia to be so visibly bothered. (Kecia) page 97

20-21) Joel 2:28-29, Acts 2:17-18 And it shall come to pass afterward, that I will pour out my Spirit upon all flesh;
and your sons and your daughters shall prophecy, your old men shall dream dreams, your young men shall see visions:
And also upon the servants and upon the handmaids in those days will I pour out my Spirit. (Given to everyone, Inspirational)

No one was immune from the impact of the staff, regardless of their station in life. (Staff) page 9

"Matthew could predict with certainty that whether the letter was sent to you by his commanding officer or he returned and gifted it to someone who desperately needed hope, its purpose was far-reaching." (Matthew) page 48

When Rhesa announced the direction of her future with such confidence, Kecia understood the encounter she had had. (Kecia, Rhesa) page 87

After returning home, Peter experienced something he had not in years. Whether awake or resting, a new dream was taking place in his soul. (Peter) page 32

For Colson, the lens provided so much more than pictures and images. It was a gift of vision to him. He could see how things used to be and should be and will be. (Colson) page 60

22) Micah 3:8 But truly I am full of power by the Spirit of the Lord, and of judgment, and of might, to declare unto Jacob his transgression, and to Israel his sin. (Empowers)

This process of studying deeply the reality of the past, with the guidance of Kecia, brought Peter an overwhelming sense of clarity and ability to address his industry in particular and business as a whole. (Kecia, Peter) page 29

23-24) Zechariah 12:10 And I will pour upon the house of David, and upon the inhabitants of Jerusalem, the Spirit of grace and of supplications. (Provides for unmerited favor, Provides for prayer)

He wondered what he ever could have done to deserve the hours Aaron spent pouring into his life and found himself wanting to do the same for others. (Aaron, Colson) page 73

Ragan was mesmerized listening to her pray and found her own prayers transformed in her presence. (Kecia, Ragan) page 99

25) Matthew 3:16 And Jesus, when he was baptized, went up straightway out of the water: and, lo, the heavens were opened unto him, and he saw the Spirit of God descending like a dove, and lighting upon him. (Transforms)

Colson often saw in the smallest creature the opportunity for something larger than life. (Colson) page 60

26) Matthew 10:20 For it is not ye that speak but the Spirit of your Father which speaketh in you. (Speaks through people)

Often when Adlai couldn't find words to say how she was feeling, she repeated some of the things Kecia had told her. (Kecia, Adlai) page 39

27) Matthew 12:28 But if I cast out devils by the Spirit of God, then the kingdom of God is come unto you. (Performs miracles)

She recognized the miracle of the darkness that was gone after one of the most intense evenings she and Kecia had spent together. (Kecia, Ragan) page 99

28) Matthew 12:31-32 Wherefore I say unto you, all manner of sin and blasphemy shall be forgiven unto men: but the blasphemy against the Holy Ghost shall not be forgiven unto men.
And whosoever speaketh a word against the Son of Man, it shall be forgiven him: but whosoever speaketh against the Holy Ghost, it shall not be forgiven him, neither in this world, neither in the world to come. (Eternal consequences for sinning against)

Aaron explained that what had been done was unforgivable, and the outcome would be far-reaching. (Aaron) page 62

29) Matthew 28:19 Go ye therefore and teach all nations, baptizing them in the name of the Father, and of the Son, and of the Holy Ghost. (Trinity)

The owner, editor, and staff were solidly cohesive. (Team) page 8

30) Luke 1:15 For he shall be great in the sight of the Lord, and shall drink neither wine nor strong drink; and he shall be filled with the Holy Ghost, even from his mother's womb. (Fills)

"Matthew just seemed saturated with good." (Matthew) page 48

31) Luke 1:35 And the angel answered and said unto her, The Holy Ghost shall come upon thee, and the power of the Highest shall overshadow thee: therefore also that holy thing which shall be born of thee shall be called the Son of God. (Omnipotent)

Something that seemed impossible to everyone, they could orchestrate. (Staff) page 8

32) Luke 1:41 And it came to pass, when Elizabeth heard the salutation of Mary, the babe leaped in her womb; and Elizabeth was filled with the Holy Ghost. (Fills)

Every place she touched became permeated with joy. (Kecia) page 13

33) Luke 1:67 And his father Zechariah was filled with the Holy Ghost, and prophesied, saying. (Fills)

He ushered in a sense of hope for the future. (Aaron) page 9

34) Luke 4:1 And Jesus being full of the Holy Ghost returned from Jordan, and was led by the Spirit into the wilderness. (Fills)

Garrick was delighted to be with Kecia and Aaron as they transitioned into this phase. They were with him at a critical juncture. (Editor, Staff) page 8

35) Luke 4:17-19 And there was delivered unto him the book of the prophet Isaiah. And when he had opened the book, he found the place where it was written,
The Spirit of the Lord is upon me, because he hath anointed me to preach the gospel to the poor; he hath sent me to heal the broken-hearted, to preach deliverance to the captives, and recovering of sight to the blind, to set at liberty them that are bruised,
to preach the acceptable year of the Lord. (Anoints)

Before Garrick released the group back to their life outside the museum, he read from one of his many favorite books, Isaiah. "I'm so taken with the presence of the Trinity. I am blessed to offer this gift to everyone. I am here to fix broken hearts and broken bodies. Issues and people do not hold you captive. Everything that matters is here." (Team, Adlai, Colson, Matthew, Matthew's parents, Miron, Peter and Amy, Ragan, Rhesa) page 142

36-37) John 3:5-8 Jesus answered, verily, verily, I say unto thee, except a man be born of water and of the Spirit, he cannot enter into the kingdom of God.

That which is born of the flesh is flesh; and that which is born of the Spirit is Spirit.

Marvel not that I said unto thee, ye must be born again.

The wind bloweth where it listeth, and thou hearest the sound thereof, but canst not tell whence it cometh, and whither it goeth: so is every one that is born of the Spirit. (Restorative, Mysterious)

Kecia was all about the stuff that lasts. She had a way with life and rubbed off on everyone around her, with this uncanny ability to flit in and out of lives at the right time. (Kecia) page 13

38-39) John 7:38-39 He that believeth on me, as the Scripture hath said, out of his belly shall flow rivers of living waters.

But this spake he of the Spirit, which they that believe on him should receive: for the Holy Ghost was not yet given; because that Jesus was not yet glorified. (Life-giving, Given to earth)

When she felt empty, Ragan remembered Kecia telling her that her faith was the source of constant, overflowing life. (Kecia, Ragan) page 92

The plan had been in place for years, but when the timing was right, Garrick spoke to his colleagues about additional personnel. He then could be promoted to editor. (Editor, Staff) page 7

40-41) John 14:16-18 And I will pray the Father, and he shall give you another Comforter, that he may abide with you forever;

Even the Spirit of truth, whom the world cannot receive, because it seeth him not, neither knoweth him, but ye know him for he dwelleth with you, and shall be in you.
I will not leave you comfortless: I will come to you. (Comfort, Truth)

The archivist in him was so concerned with the preservation of the collection, he talked to the owner about employing staff who would take great care with the truth for each piece. They would provide support and stay with the story ad infinitum. Manipulation of facts had become so prevalent, it was hard to recognize sincerity. Garrick's work could be trusted to be without embellishment. It didn't need it. It was important that he provide that reassurance through personnel. (Team) page 7

42-44) John 14:26 But the Comforter, which is the Holy Ghost, whom the Father will send in my name, he shall teach you all things, and bring all things to your remembrance, whatsoever I have said unto you. (Comforts, Teaches, Reminds)

Kecia and Aaron immediately were part of the organization. Each provided multiple skills and took on several roles and had a quality that seemed incomprehensible. Kecia had a presence about her that granted a place of solace. Aaron's gifts included thorough instruction and the ability to prompt a memory and direct it to the answer. (Team) page 8

45-50) John 16:7-15 Nevertheless I tell you the truth; it is expedient for you that I go away: for if I go not away, the Comforter will not come unto you; but if I depart, I will send him unto you.

And when he is come, he will reprove the world of sin, and of righteousness, and of judgment:

Of sin, because they believe not on me;

Of righteousness, because I go to my Father, and ye see me no more;

Of judgment, because the prince of this world is judged.

I have yet many things to say unto you, but ye cannot bear them now.

Howbeit when he, the Spirit of truth, is come, he will guide you into all truth: for he shall not speak of himself, but whatsoever he shall hear, that shall he speak; and he will show you things to come.

He shall glorify me: for he shall receive of mine, and shall show it unto you.

All things that the Father hath are mine: therefore said I, that he shall take of mine, and shall show it unto you. (Arrives, Convinces, Guides, Speaks, Reveals, Glorifies)

With more support in the field and Garrick as editor, the staff was an incredible reflection of his strength. (Editor, Staff) page 8

When Kecia said with confidence that everything wrong hinges on lack of faith, her words pierced Ragan. How could she establish so much in such a non-condemning way? (Kecia, Ragan) page 99

Kecia was very persuasive, but she truly won Rhesa over to the idea when she said, "With the writing and editing, how could this story not have merit? Not to mention the facilities and resources and business model and countless hours from the dedicated team members." (Kecia, Rhesa) page 87

Ragan could spend the whole evening with her and not hear one critical, judgmental remark. When she asked her how she had acquired this skill, Kecia responded, "The best of us is judged. The rest don't need to be." (Kecia, Ragan) page 92

Just her presence brought out Peter's ability to see the truth. (Kecia, Peter) page 31

Adlai glowed when Kecia told her that these words came directly from the owner of the museum. (Team, Adlai) page 43

"Kecia and Aaron have given you a glimpse into something that you long for, heaven." (Editor, Staff, Adlai, Colson, Matthew's parents, Miron, Peter and Amy, Ragan, Rhesa) page 124

They drew upon his character and represented him well. The reputation of the owner naturally flowed to the editor. (Team) page 8, 8

51) Acts 1:16 Men and brethren, this Scripture must needs have been fulfilled, which the Holy Ghost by the mouth of David spake before concerning Judas, which was guide to them that took Jesus. (Speaks through people)

The message Aaron portrayed was powerful, and it came out clearly through Matthew's words. (Aaron, Matthew) page 50

52) Acts 2:4 And they were all filled with the Holy Ghost, and began to speak with other tongues, as the Spirit gave them utterance. (Fills)

They were all so enamored with the gift that had been given to them, they knew they would never look or sound the same again.

(Staff, Adlai, Colson, Matthew, Matthew's parents, Miron, Peter and Amy, Ragan, Rhesa) page 141

53) Acts 2:33 Therefore being by the right hand of God exalted, and having received of the Father the promise of the Holy Ghost, he hath shed forth this, which ye now see and hear. (Promised)

Since Garrick was in his ultimate role and now physically located at the museum, he had the owner's blessing to send the staff to the field. (Team) page 7

54) Acts 2:38 Then Peter said unto them, repent, and be baptized every one of you in the name of Jesus Christ for the remission of sins, and ye shall receive the gift of the Holy Ghost. (Received upon faith)

Access to staff was simple because of the work already done by the editor. (Editor, Staff) page 8

55) Acts 4:8 Then Peter, filled with the Holy Ghost, said unto them, ye rulers of the people, and elders of Israel. (Fills)

Even though he was very young, he had a spirit of authority about him. (Matthew) page 48

56) Acts 5:3-4 But Peter said, Ananias, why hath Satan filled thine heart to lie to the Holy Ghost, and to keep back part of the price of the land? While it remained, was it not thine own? And after it was sold, was it not in thine own power? Why has thou conceived this thing in thine heart? Thou hast not lied unto men but unto God. (One with God)

In all their work, the title of staff commanded the same respect as that of the owner. (Owner, Staff) page 8

57-58) Acts 5:32 And we are his witnesses of these things; and so is also the Holy Ghost, whom God hath given to them that obey him. (Witness, Gift to the obedient)

A sense of pride overwhelmed Aaron as he spoke. "I can attest to the change in Matthew." (Aaron, Matthew) page 48

"I know how hard you've tried to follow God's intention. Let me help you get through this." (Aaron, Miron) page 108

59-61) Acts 6:3-5 Wherefore, brethren, look ye out among you seven men of honest report, full of the Holy Ghost and wisdom, whom we may appoint over this business.
But we will give ourselves continually to prayer, and to the ministry of the word.
And the saying pleased the whole multitude: and they chose Stephen, a man full of faith and of the Holy Ghost, and Philip, and Prochorus, and Nicanor, and Timon, and Parmenas, and Nicolas a proselyte of Antioch. (Honest reputation, Wisdom, Faith)

Colson was determined to follow Aaron's example and be known for his integrity at the purest level. (Aaron, Colson) page 64

Ragan's understanding of people and the intricacies of life grew every time she listened to Kecia. (Kecia, Ragan) page 91

It would be easy for Adlai to believe in the incredible universe, especially after taking in everything Kecia had to show her. (Kecia, Adlai) page 39

62) Acts 7:51 Ye stiffnecked and uncircumcised in heart and ears, ye do always resist the Holy Ghost: as your fathers did, so do ye. (Resisted)

She had a grasp on the situation but received so much defiance and friction, there was no opportunity to talk about all of the people he was negatively affecting with his take-over. (Kecia) page 29

63) Acts 7:55 But he, being full of the Holy Ghost, looked up steadfastly into heaven, and saw the glory of God, and Jesus standing on the right hand of God. (Fills)

Colson was completely lost in their expression of love, was stable in his gaze but trembled too much to photograph anything when he saw the Jenski he had heard so much about, its brilliant owner, and his trusted editor standing next to him, both anxiously waiting to welcome everyone. (Team, Adlai, Colson, Matthew's parents, Miron, Peter and Amy, Ragan, Rhesa) page 121

64) Acts 8:29 Then the Spirit said unto Philip, go near, and join thyself to this chariot. (Directs)

Kecia told her to reflect on her thoughts and circumstances and they would talk about it at their next dinner. (Kecia, Ragan) page 94

65) Acts 9:31 Then had the churches rest throughout all Judea and Galilee and Samaria, and were edified; and walking in the fear of the Lord, and in the comfort of the Holy Ghost, were multiplied. (Comforts)

Before meeting Kecia, for such a long time Rhesa felt nothing but alone. She now felt a part of something she still didn't fully understand, but it was encouraging, respectful, comforting, and fruitful. (Kecia, Rhesa) page 86

66) Acts 10:45 And they of the circumcision which believed were astonished, as many as came with Peter, because that on the Gentiles also was poured out the gift of the Holy Ghost. (Nondiscriminatory)

"Aaron and Kecia have been your teacher and comforter, but they are not just for a chosen few, nor are they given to the spiritually elite, whether self-defined or by the world's standards. The spirit is for all mankind." (Owner, Staff, Adlai, Colson, Matthew's parents, Miron, Peter and Amy, Ragan, Rhesa) page 125

67) Acts 11:24 For he was a good man, and full of the Holy Ghost and of faith: and much people was added unto the Lord. (Fills)

"He had a pure heart and was never empty when it came to his convictions. His faith was contagious." (Matthew) page 48

68) Acts 13:2-4 As they ministered to the Lord, and fasted, the Holy Ghost said, separate me Barnabas and Saul for the work whereunto I have called them.

And when they had fasted and prayed, and laid their hands on them, they sent them away.
So they, being sent forth by the Holy Ghost, departed unto Seleucia, and from then they sailed to Cyprus. (Commissions)

The staff explained they all had been selected not just for an adventure or even a season of personal growth but for a lifetime of worship. The tasks they would undertake in their daily lives, whether joyous or heavy, and the relationships they would nurture would bless the team. They were not dismissed from the Jenski; they were appointed by the spirit. (Team, Adlai, Colson, Matthew, Matthew's parents, Miron, Peter and Amy, Ragan, Rhesa) page 141

69) Acts 13:9 Then Saul, [who also is called Paul,] filled with the Holy Ghost, set his eyes on him. (Fills)

Peter was replete with the ideology he and Kecia had discussed as he confronted the owner of the company that solicited his competitor. (Kecia, Peter) page 29

70) Acts 13:52 And the disciples were filled with joy, and with the Holy Ghost. (Fills)

Simply being near her generated a festive mood. (Staff, Adlai, Colson, Matthew's parents, Miron, Peter and Amy, Ragan, Rhesa) page 121

71) Acts 20:22-23 And now, behold, I go bound in the spirit unto Jerusalem, not knowing the things that shall befall me there:
Save that the Holy Ghost witnesseth in every city, saying that bonds and afflictions abide me. (Witnesses)

"He stated that he was drawn to this mission even without knowing what it would entail. I affirmed to him that it would be difficult." (Aaron, Matthew) page 48

72) Acts 20:28 Take heed thereof unto yourselves, and to all the flock, over the which the Holy Ghost hath made you overseers, to feed the church of God, which he hath purchased with his own blood. (Chooses leaders)

This encounter changed their direction. Each of them would find themselves in a place of influence with the ability to care for others who also had been captured by the author's love. (Team, Adlai, Colson, Matthew, Matthew's parents, Miron, Peter and Amy, Ragan, Rhesa) page 142

73) Acts 28:25 And when they agreed not among themselves, they departed, after that Paul had spoken one word, Well spake the Holy Ghost by Isaiah the prophet unto our fathers. (Speaks through prophets)

Kecia believed that ministers conveyed the message to those who needed it. (Kecia) page 96

74) Romans 1:4 And declared to be the Son of God with power, according to the Spirit of holiness, by the resurrection from the dead. (Holy)

I have listened intently to the reverence in speaking of the Beloved Soldier. (Matthew) page 52

75) Romans 8:2 For the law of the Spirit of life in Christ Jesus hath made me free from the law of sin and death. (Frees)

It is all completely liberating. (Matthew) page 53

76-77) Romans 8:9 But ye are not in the flesh, but in the Spirit, if so be that the Spirit of God dwell in you. Now if any man have not the Spirit of Christ, he is none of his. (Unburdens, Accompanies)

She was enjoying a lot of still rather new freedoms. Matters she used to consider important were no longer when she truly searched her heart. (Ragan) page 99

It was understood they were a package deal. (Editor, Staff) page 8

78-79) Romans 8:11 But if the Spirit of him that raised up Jesus from the dead dwell in you, he that raised up Christ from the dead shall also quicken your mortal bodies by his Spirit that dwelleth in you. (Resurrects, Indwells)

Kecia and Aaron knew if they became a part of these lives, they would have the same life-restoring impact they had once had with Garrick. (Editor, Staff) page 9

80-83) Romans 8:13-16 For if ye live after the flesh, ye shall die: but if ye through the Spirit do mortify the deeds of the body, ye shall live.
For as many as are led by the Spirit of God, they are the sons of God.

For ye have not received the spirit of bondage again to fear; but ye have received the Spirit of adoption, whereby we cry, Abba, Father.

The Spirit itself beareth witness with our spirit, that we are the children of God. (Subdues, Leads descendants, Adopts, Bears witness)

She now had the tenacity and vision to change her definition of life. (Kecia, Ragan) page 99

He told them all that they had been compelled by his spirit to be there because they already belonged. (Owner, Staff, Adlai, Colson, Matthew's parents, Miron, Peter and Amy, Ragan, Rhesa) page 133

"This will not enslave me or consume me. I've been embraced by my father." (Owner, Staff, Miron) page 112

"It will be infinitely visible to you through this experience that you are my very own." (Owner, Staff, Adlai, Colson, Matthew's parents, Miron, Peter and Amy, Ragan, Rhesa) page 125

84-85) Romans 8:26 Likewise the Spirit also helpeth our infirmities: for we know not what we should pray for as we ought: but the Spirit itself maketh intercession for us with groanings which cannot be uttered. (Helps our infirmities, Intercedes)

"I don't know what to pray anymore. I know you've gone to bat for me. Words can't express the awesome advocate you are." (Aaron, Miron) page 108

86) Romans 14:17 For the kingdom of God is not meat and drink; but righteousness, and peace, and joy in the Holy Ghost. (Offers righteousness, peace, and joy)

Too much of his life had been spent toiling when goodness and rest and great happiness is so readily available. (Peter) page 32

87) Romans 15:16 That I should be the minister of Jesus Christ to the Gentiles, ministering the gospel of God, that the offering up of the Gentiles might be acceptable, being sanctified by the Holy Ghost. (Sanctifies)

"Your lives have been perfectly edited by my son and completely refined by my spirit." (Team, Adlai, Colson, Matthew's parents, Miron, Peter and Amy, Ragan, Rhesa) page 125

88-93) 1 Corinthians 2:10-14 But God hath revealed them unto us by his Spirit: for the Spirit searcheth all things, yea, the deep things of God.
For what man knoweth the things of a man, save the spirit of man which is in him? Even so the things of God knoweth no man, but the Spirit of God.
Now we have received, not the spirit of the world, but the Spirit which is of God; that we might know the things that are freely given to us of God.
Which things also we speak, not in the words which man's wisdom teacheth, but which the Holy Ghost teacheth; comparing spiritual things with spiritual.
But the natural man receiveth not the things of the Spirit of God: for they are foolishness unto him: neither can he know them,

because they are spiritually discerned. (Enlightens, Explores, Omniscient, Informs, Teaches, Gives discernment)

She was too excited to wait to share details of the incredible day they would travel to the Jenski Museum with the rest of the group to experience history in the making. (Owner, Kecia, Adlai) page 41

Kecia had pursued every morsel of information to the finest detail that the owner had in place. She did so in order to impart this to everyone. (Owner, Kecia) page 41

The staff knew everything there was to know about the owner, his dreams and intentions and vision. (Owner, Staff) page 8

"You're too smart to fill your head with that noise. You need time without the clutter to listen to nothing but the wind and understand how rich your life is." (Kecia, Rhesa) page 80

I know it may not seem logical for me to think this way, and I understand how this might encourage criticism. This isn't from a textbook, protocol, or guideline, but I've learned to listen to a source that is scholarly and unlike anything I've ever known. (Matthew) page 52

Her ability to perceive beyond the obvious and ordinary matured as they spent time together exploring every topic important to them. (Kecia, Ragan) page 91

94-99) I Corinthians 12:3-13 Wherefore I give you to understand, that no man speaking by the Spirit of God calleth

Jesus accursed: and that no man can say that Jesus is the Lord, but by the Holy Ghost.

Now there are diversities of gifts, but the same Spirit.

And there are differences of administrations, but the same Lord.

And there are diversities of operations, but it is the same God which worketh all in all.

But the manifestation of the Spirit is given to every man to profit withal.

For to one is given by the Spirit the word of wisdom; to another the word of knowledge by the same Spirit;

To another faith by the same Spirit; to another the gifts of healing by the same Spirit;

To another the working of miracles; to another prophecy; to another discerning of spirits; to another divers kinds of tongues; to another the interpretation of tongues:

But all these worketh that one and the selfsame Spirit, dividing to every man severally as he will.

For as the body is one, and hath many members, and all the members of that one body, being many, are one body: so also is Christ.

For by one Spirit are we all baptized into one body, whether we be Jews or Gentiles, whether we be bond or free; and have been all made to drink into one Spirit. (Restrains and releases, Bestows, Displays, Gives, Apportions, Connects)

Dad, I know there are many industries that promote this tough language, and obviously in my youth I would not have been able to hold back my words, but now I feel liberated to speak only my faith. (Matthew) page 52

The staff had selected gifts unique to each one of them. This would assist them in their distinct service for the team. The owner would accomplish awesome plans in and through their lives. (Team, Adlai, Colson, Matthew, Matthew's parents, Miron, Peter and Amy, Ragan, Rhesa) page 138

Staff would assure their days would be so rich that everyone around them would benefit as well. (Staff, Adlai, Colson, Matthew, Matthew's parents, Miron, Peter and Amy, Ragan, Rhesa) page 138

"Your gift is insight. It will guide your heart and change your life." page 139

Aaron instructed his student once again, "Your gift is not limited to a single course of study. Your philosophy will be broad and extensive and will carry you through difficult decisions." page 139

The symbol was given to him by his parents, but it was the spirit who gave him the gift of faith. page 139

"Your gift is healing. You've been honored to experience some of the pain of the editor and understand how even the most remote parts of the body die without a constant flow of blood. Though this season has felt like repetitive injury to your body and soul, there is redemptive healing through the spirit." page 141

"You will see miracles all around you and be involved in their spectacle." page 138

"This now becomes your symbol, and your gift is speech. You have a story to tell in a manner that will be received." page 140

"Your gift is intuition. You will distinguish between truth and deception." page 140

Kecia stated, "Love is the symbol. Your gift is language, and Amy will facilitate." page 141

(Staff, Adlai, Colson, Matthew, Matthew's parents, Miron, Peter and Amy, Ragan, Rhesa)

Kecia and Aaron entrusted all these attributes to these souls they had followed intently. (Staff, Adlai, Colson, Matthew, Matthew's parents, Miron, Peter and Amy, Ragan, Rhesa) page 141

Kecia told her she was thinking about how much Garrick adores this stuff, the fact that all of these individuals came from separate circumstances and are now here together learning about each other and how their paths have crossed. (Editor, Staff, Adlai, Colson, Matthew's parents, Miron, Peter and Amy, Ragan, Rhesa) page 121

100) 2 Corinthians 13:14 The grace of the Lord Jesus Christ and the love of God, and the communion of the Holy Ghost, be with you all. Amen. (Communes)

"Take with you our blessing, our heart, and our presence." (Team, Adlai, Colson, Matthew, Matthew's parents, Miron, Peter and Amy, Ragan, Rhesa) page 142

101) Galatians 4:6 And because ye are sons, God hath sent forth the Spirit of his Son into your hearts, crying, Abba, Father. (Aligns)

"The editor is the owner's son, and you are the owner's children as well. He sent us to be with you. The owner is your author, but you may also address him as dad." (Team, Adlai, Colson, Matthew's parents, Miron, Peter and Amy, Ragan, Rhesa) page 124

102-103) Galatians 5:16-18 This I say then, Walk in the Spirit, and ye shall not fulfill the lust of the flesh.

For the flesh lusteth against the Spirit, and the Spirit against the flesh: and these are contrary the one to the other: so that ye cannot do the things that ye would.

But if ye be led of the Spirit, ye are not under the law. (Prohibits, Simplifies)

If she focused on the truth, she could let things go that are harmful yet somehow are also compelling. A lie evokes this emotion, and evil can be alluring still when good is right next to it. It's debilitating. When reality wins, restrictions aren't necessary. (Ragan) page 98

104) Galatians 5:22-23 But the fruit of the Spirit is love, joy, peace, long-suffering, gentleness, goodness, faith, meekness, temperance: against such there is no law. (Bears fruit)

Part of the result of all this for Rhesa was a new definition of love. All she could do was display it because she sure couldn't explain it. (Rhesa) page 86

If you could somehow test it on a happiness meter, the cheerfulness left in her wake was off the chart. (Kecia) page 13

At even the slightest glance, the contentment that had been missing so long in his life was clearly evident on Peter's face. (Peter) page 32

Miron was in it for the long haul. (Miron) page 106

As lively as Adlai was, she could also be very gentle. (Adlai) page 37

Colson was just a good kid. (Colson) page 59

"Matthew believed with every fiber in him that this was ultimately what he was to do with the rest of his life." (Matthew) page 46

Aaron's character served him well in this role. He quietly went about his work without unnecessary confrontation or a combative attitude. (Aaron) page 9

Kecia saw great hope in a newfound ability to let things go that used to gnaw at her. There was no rule that said she had to carry that load. (Kecia, Ragan) page 99

105) Ephesians 1:17 That the God of our Lord Jesus Christ, the Father of glory, may give unto you the Spirit of wisdom and revelation in the knowledge of him. (Reveals)

Listening to Kecia talk about principles caused Ragan to be in a place where she had never been. It was this strange mix of being a child learning for the first time and soaking it all in to a maturity level well beyond yesterday. (Kecia, Ragan) page 92

106) Ephesians 3:16 That he would grant you, according to the riches of his glory, to be strengthened with might by his Spirit in the inner man. (Strengthens)

"Every parent desires that their child be gifted with incredible, unending courage that completely envelops who they are." (Colson) page 69

107) Ephesians 4:30 And grieve not the holy Spirit of God, whereby ye are sealed unto the day of redemption. (Upholds)

I want to live without regret, knowing that I am accountable only to the one who calls my name at the rescue mission that counts. (Matthew) page 53

108) Ephesians 6:17 And take the helmet of salvation, and the sword of the Spirit, which is the word of God. (Engages)

I have every weapon I need in the eternal war of good over evil. (Matthew) page 56

109) 2 Thessalonians 2:13 But we are bound to give thanks always to God for you, brethren beloved of the Lord, because God hath from the beginning chosen you to salvation through sanctification of the Spirit and belief of the truth. (Atones)

"Your lives are treasured because you have always belonged here with us. Your membership has been donated and your trust in the organization acknowledged." (Team, Adlai, Colson, Matthew's parents, Miron, Peter and Amy, Ragan, Rhesa) page 124

110) 1 Timothy 3:16 And without controversy great is the mystery of godliness: God was manifest in the flesh, justified in the Spirit, seen of angels, preached unto the Gentiles, believed on in the world, received up into glory. (Justifies)

"This holiness is a conundrum. I know it's been taken care of for me, presented, affirmed and confirmed, taught and accepted, delivered." (Ragan) page 100

111) Hebrews 9:14 How much more shall the blood of Christ, who through the eternal Spirit offered himself without spot to God, purge your conscience from dead works to serve the living God? (Sustains)

Miron spoke for all of the chosen when he stated, "We will always remember how the team provided for our stories so we could be unburdened with what is only temporary and focus on our eternal destiny." (Team, Adlai, Colson, Matthew, Matthew's parents, Miron, Peter and Amy, Ragan, Rhesa) page 142

112) Hebrews 10:15 Whereof the Holy Ghost also is a witness to us: for after that he had said before. (Witnesses)

When they relayed information, there was no doubting its validity. Their word was solid. (Staff) page 8

113) 1 Peter 4:14 If ye be reproached for the name of Christ, happy are ye; for the Spirit of glory and of God resteth upon you. (Honors)

"It doesn't matter, if it's for the right reason. The outcome is actually positive. It will be obvious who's on your side." (Kecia, Ragan) page 93

114) 1 John 2:20, 27 But ye have an unction from the Holy One, and ye know all things.

But the anointing which ye have received of him abideth in you, and ye need not that any man teach you: but as the same anointing teacheth you of all things, and is truth, and is no lie, and even as it hath taught you, ye shall abide in him. (Anoints)

"You've been blessed, and your perception is good. This will remain with you. You don't have to look to other sources. This is your place of rest." (Kecia, Rhesa) page 87

115) 1 John 4:1-6 Beloved, believe not every spirit, but try the spirits whether they are of God: because many false prophets are gone out into the world.
Hereby know ye the Spirit of God: every spirit that confesseth that Jesus Christ is come in the flesh is of God:
and every spirit that confesseth not that Jesus Christ is come in the flesh is not of God: and this is that spirit of anti-christ, whereof ye have heard that it should come; and even now already is it in the world.
Ye are of God, little children, and have overcome them: because greater is he that is in you, than he that is in the world.
They are of the world: therefore speak they of the world, and the world heareth them.
We are of God: he that knoweth God heareth us: he that is not of God heareth not us.
Hereby know we the Spirit of truth, and the spirit of error. (Gives discernment)

"There are things you should question. A lot of people try to claim something is virtuous when it's their own agenda they are trying to promote. Bottom line, it shouldn't conflict with your faith, but there's a destructive mindset out there that I believe will get worse. That's all in the past for you. You have something

greater now. It's substance over fluff, certainty over fallacy."
(Kecia, Ragan) page 93

116) Revelation 19:10 And I fell at his feet to worship him. And
he said unto me, See thou do it not: I am thy fellow servant, and
of thy brethren that have the testimony of Jesus: worship God:
for the testimony of Jesus is the Spirit of prophecy. (Prophesies
Jesus)

They would speak always about the incredible artistry the editor
would bring to a story. (Editor, Staff) page 8

Appendix G: Answers to B

001) Accompanies	77
002) Adopts	82
003) Affirms the Creator	18
004) Aligns	101
005) Anoints	35
006) Anoints	114
007) Apportions	98
008) Arrives	45
009) Atones	109
010) Bears fruit	104
011) Bears witness	83
012) Belongs with God	3
013) Bestows	95
014) Cherished	8
015) Chooses leaders	72
016) Comfort	40
017) Comforts	42
018) Comforts	65
019) Commissions	68
020) Communes	100
021) Connects	99
022) Convinces	46
023) Creates	7
024) Creation	1
025) Design	13
026) Directs	64
027) Displays	96
028) Education	15

Appendix H: Answers to C

1-2	102-103
3	7
4-5	40-41
6	14
7	25
8-11	10-13
12	62
13	70
14	100
15	113
16-17	20-21
18-23	94-99
24	106
25	26
26-27	5-6
28	22
29	29
30-31	8-9
32-33	15-16
34	31
35-36	78-79
37	64
38	34
39	52
40	72
41	30
42	101
43-45	42-44
46-47	36-37

48	19
49	86
50	35
51-56	45-50
57-58	38-39
59	54
60	71
61	27
62-63	1-2
64-66	59-61
67	66
68-69	17-18
70	105
71	68
72	51
73	116
74	73
75	56
76	67
77	75
78-79	23-24
80	69
81-84	80-83
85	109
86-91	88-93
92	63
93	115
94	33
95	87
96	104
97	74
98	53

99	107
100-101	76-77
102-103	57-58
104	108
105-106	3-4
107	111
108	32
109	114
110	55
111	65
112	28
113	112
114	110
115-116	84-85